He demanded answers.

"Can I help you?" Sylvie's voice carried in soft and low tones better suited to a seductress than a murderess. Of course there was no reason she couldn't be both.

"Bryce Walker. I'm an attorney. I need to ask you some questions." His voice sounded as businesslike and detached as he'd hoped. As if he was merely doing his job for a client.

The furthest thing from the truth.

He peered through the small crack, trying to get a better look at her. Blond hair, large blue eyes, a heart-shaped face any man would enjoy seeing on the pillow beside him. She held a hand to her chest, spreading pink-polished fingers across cleavage exposed by a formal green gown.

"You are Diana Gale."

"She is my sister. She was supposed to be married today. But the wedding never took place."

She sounded sincere. Fortunately he was well aware of his typical male weakness for beautiful women. And he knew how to compensate.

ANN VOSS PETERSON

SERIAL BRIDE

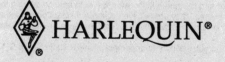

HARLEQUIN®

TORONTO • NEW YORK • LONDON
AMSTERDAM • PARIS • SYDNEY • HAMBURG
STOCKHOLM • ATHENS • TOKYO • MILAN • MADRID
PRAGUE • WARSAW • BUDAPEST • AUCKLAND

If you purchased this book without a cover you should be aware that this book is stolen property. It was reported as "unsold and destroyed" to the publisher, and neither the author nor the publisher has received any payment for this "stripped book."

To Michael Voss and Christopher Voss,
the best brothers a girl could have.

ISBN 0-373-22925-9

SERIAL BRIDE

Copyright © 2006 by Ann Voss Peterson

All rights reserved. Except for use in any review, the reproduction or utilization of this work in whole or in part in any form by any electronic, mechanical or other means, now known or hereafter invented, including xerography, photocopying and recording, or in any information storage or retrieval system, is forbidden without the written permission of the publisher, Harlequin Enterprises Limited, 225 Duncan Mill Road, Don Mills, Ontario, Canada M3B 3K9.

All characters in this book have no existence outside the imagination of the author and have no relation whatsoever to anyone bearing the same name or names. They are not even distantly inspired by any individual known or unknown to the author, and all incidents are pure invention.

This edition published by arrangement with Harlequin Books S.A.

® and TM are trademarks of the publisher. Trademarks indicated with ® are registered in the United States Patent and Trademark Office, the Canadian Trade Marks Office and in other countries.

www.eHarlequin.com

Printed in U.S.A.

ABOUT THE AUTHOR

Ever since she was a little girl making her own books out of construction paper, Ann Voss Peterson wanted to write. So when it came time to choose a major at the University of Wisconsin, creative writing was her only choice. Of course, writing wasn't a *practical* choice—one needs to earn a living. So Ann found jobs ranging from proofreading legal transcripts, to working with quarter horses, to washing windows. But no matter how she earned her paycheck, she continued to write the type of stories that captured her heart and imagination—romantic suspense. Ann lives near Madison, Wisconsin, with her husband, her two young sons, her Border collie and her quarter horse mare. Ann loves to hear from readers. E-mail her at ann@annvosspeterson.com or visit her Web site at annvosspeterson.com.

Books by Ann Voss Peterson

*Wedding Mission

CAST OF CHARACTERS

Sylvie Hayes—A survivor of the foster care system, Sylvie had always dreamed of having a family of her own. But when her long-lost twin sister disappears from her own wedding, and Sylvie's family turns out to be more nightmare than dream, who can she turn to? Who can she trust?

Bryce Walker—Convinced Sylvie's sister is a handmaiden of the serial killer responsible for his brother's death, Bryce works to win Sylvie's trust, hoping she will lead him to the missing bride. But he doesn't count on the need to protect Sylvie. Or the need to claim her for his own.

Diana Gale—Sylvie's twin sister was supposed to be walking down the aisle to marry the man she loves. Instead the bride is missing and her groom is barely clinging to life. Is she the family Sylvie has always wanted or a dangerous killer?

Detective Stan Perreth—The secretive police detective has a bad attitude. Is he working to find Diana or working to blame her for his crimes?

Dryden Kane—The serial killer has been in prison for years. Now he's anxious to settle the score.

Louis Ingersoll—Diana's neighbor would do anything for her. But does that include murder?

Professor Vincent Bertram—The professor has spent much of his life studying the grisly crimes of Dryden Kane. How far will he go to make sure his research pays off?

Sami Yamal—The professor's assistant, Sami believes he deserves credit for the professor's research. But how far will he go to prove he is the real expert?

Chapter One

Sylvie Hayes dug her polished nails into the tulle wrapping the stems of her maid-of-honor nosegay and stared down the church's long aisle. A blend of alstroemeria and autumn chrysanthemums smothered the altar. Faces peered expectantly from pews, a sea of humanity tied back with white lacy bows. The organ soared into Bach, rattling stained glass like thunder from an approaching storm—the cue to start her measured march down the aisle.

Where was Diana?

Her sister had said she needed a moment to check her makeup, to make sure everything was perfect for her wedding. But that had been over fifteen minutes ago. She should be back by now.

And where was the groom?

Sylvie squinted at the shadows to the side of the altar. Although she spotted the minister and best man, she couldn't see Reed McCaskey anywhere.

Sylvie and Diana might not know one another as well as twins who'd grown up in the same household, but since Diana had tracked her down six months ago, they had become close. Closer than Sylvie had dared to get to another person. And even though Diana's marriage would probably change things, she felt the connection they shared, the sense of the other she'd heard about in twins, would never go away. She'd feel an unexplained twinge of joy before Diana even had a chance to call her about good news. An insistent hum in the back of her mind when Diana was in trouble. That hum had been building to a crescendo over the past three months. Now it threatened to drown out the organ.

Sylvie turned away from the mouth of the nave and started down the long hall leading to the lounge where she and Diana had dressed for the wedding. She had to find her sister. She had to make sure Diana was okay.

Her heels clacked on the marble floor, matching the thump of her pulse. No doubt Diana was wrestling with her veil or some other detail. Or maybe she and Reed had argued. Whatever had happened, the alarm buzzing low in Sylvie's ears was due to an overactive imagination. Nothing more.

She quickened her pace.

She pushed her way into the lounge. The room appeared just as they'd left it. Makeup cases and dress bags cluttered the tables and draped to the floor. Photos from an instant camera smiled from a pile on one of the sofas. The spice of perfume still hung in the air.

But no Diana.

Was she preening in front of the mirror in the adjoining restroom? Sylvie crossed the lounge and opened the door. The vanity was vacant, the wide mirror catching no reflection but her own—a slip of seafoam satin, a fall of blond hair, the gleam of worry in light-blue eyes.

She ripped her gaze from the image and peered down the row of bathroom stalls. "Diana?" Her voice echoed off the white tile.

She gathered her gown in a fist. Bending low, she looked under the stalls. A wisp of white touched the floor in the large stall at the end, a dark shadow behind it. "Diana? Are you okay?"

Only the organ answered, its bass tones trembling through walls and centering deep in Sylvie's chest. She straightened and stepped down the row of bathroom stalls. Reaching the end, she grasped the handle and pulled.

A body lay face against the wall. Wetness glistened in black hair and trailed down the back of the tux. Motionless fingers clutched Diana's veil, the antique lace red with blood.

"Reed. Oh, my God, Reed!" She knelt beside

him. Slipping her hand along the side of his throat, she felt for a pulse.

A thready beat drummed against her fingertips.

He was alive. Thank God, he was alive. But he needed help. He needed an ambulance.

And Diana. Where was Diana?

The hum in her ears roared loud as a freight train bearing down.

Chapter Two

Sylvie watched the paramedics wheel the stretcher down the long church hall and out to the waiting ambulance. Reed was still unconscious. The white sheet cupped around him as if he was a child tucked into bed. Thick black straps hugged him to the gurney.

She wrapped her arms around her own middle, trying to warm herself, trying to feel strong. Stains marred the long seafoam silk of her gown, rust-colored smudges of Reed's blood.

"You're the one who found him?" a cigarette-roughened voice asked from behind her.

She turned around and faced a man with hard eyes and the jowls of a bulldog. "Excuse me?"

He let out an impatient sigh. "I need you to answer some questions for me. I'm in charge of this case. Detective Stan Perreth."

Her stomach lurched. She'd never met Perreth, not in the flesh, but she'd heard enough stories about him to inspire a bout of nausea. On one of her first visits to Madison, the detective had hauled Reed in front of a review committee for a punch Reed had delivered when Perreth's wife, a 911 dispatcher, had come to work with a battered face and a walking-into-a-doorknob explanation. Bad blood ran deep between the two men. And Perreth was now in charge of finding out who had attacked Reed and taken Diana?

"The first officer to the scene said you found Reed McCaskey."

Sylvie forced a deep breath. Surely Perreth could see beyond the bad blood. Surely he would do his job despite his personal feelings. "Yes. I found him when I went to check on my sister."

"Did you touch anything? Move anything?"

She thought back, trying to reconstruct what she'd done. "I checked his pulse. I ran out into the lounge. I went through Diana's bag to find her cell phone." And she'd grabbed her own purse. Had she touched anything else? She couldn't remember.

He held out a hand. "Give me the phone."

Sylvie looked down. Sure enough, the phone was still clenched in her fingers. She handed it to Perreth.

Perreth gripped it gingerly, his hands encased in clear plastic gloves. "Did your sister voice any doubts about this wedding?"

"No. I don't think so, anyway. She's been looking

forward to marrying Reed as long as I've known her."

"Did she and McCaskey have a fight?"

"A fight?"

"I'm trying to figure out what happened here this afternoon. Answer the question, please."

"There was no fight. They were both excited about the wedding. Anxious to get married."

"Anxious." He scribbled the word in his notebook.

Sylvie had an uneasy feeling about where he was heading. "You're taking this wrong. They were happy. They loved each other. They were eager to be together, to start their new life."

He nodded, but she got the feeling he was still concentrating on the word anxious.

Had she chosen that word subconsciously? Maybe she had. Diana *had* been anxious the past few months. But not about her love for Reed. Not about her marriage. At least, not that Sylvie was aware of. "I don't think you're understanding me."

He glanced up at her from under bushy brows. "Oh?"

"Diana and Reed were in love. They wanted to get married."

"Did you notice any tension between them recently?"

Back to the same track. Like a bulldog worrying over a bone. "Between them? No."

"But you noticed tension."

What was she supposed to say? She couldn't lie. "Diana seemed tense about something, yes. But not about her marriage."

He nodded, but she wasn't at all sure he had heard what she said. Not all of it, anyway.

"Where does your sister live?"

"She has an apartment on Pinckney Street. In the old Mueller building."

"Apartment number?"

"Three B."

He jotted it down. "Good, we'll get a warrant and take a look."

Unease niggled at the back of her neck with the force of a toothy bite. "If looking in Diana's apartment will help find her, I can let you in."

"Do you live with her?"

"No. I'm just visiting for the wedding." She'd been considering moving to Madison. To live near her sister. She could just as easily wait tables up here. Or maybe get a more fulfilling job. But she hadn't yet taken the plunge. "Diana gave me a key, though."

"No good. You don't have legal standing."

"Legal standing?"

"We need permission from someone with legal standing."

"Why?" The buzz in Sylvie's ears grew, making

it hard to think. The only time she'd heard the term *legal standing* was on an episode of *Law & Order.* And then it had been used to argue the admissibility of evidence—evidence used against someone charged with murder. "You think Diana did this? You think she hurt Reed?"

He held up a hand as if to shield himself from her hysteria. "I don't draw conclusions until I finish looking at the evidence."

"It sounds like you're drawing a conclusion to me. A wrong conclusion."

"I assure you that's not the case." He looked down at his notes. "But there was a history of abuse in your sister's adopted family, isn't that correct?"

"What are you getting at?"

"They say women who are abused as children often choose men who—"

"Hold on right there. You think Reed hit Diana?"

The detective stared at her, a smug look in his deep-set eyes. "Like I said, I'm still looking at the evidence. But there's a good chance your sister isn't to blame, no matter what happened. There's a chance she was merely defending herself."

She couldn't believe what she was hearing. "That's your story, not Reed's and Diana's."

Bushy brows lowered over hard eyes.

She shouldn't have said anything. And now that the words had left her lips, she couldn't bite them back.

Footsteps approached from down the hall. A uniformed officer stopped behind Perreth. "Detective?"

"Can it wait?"

"I think you're going to want to see this."

Detective Perreth's mouth twisted into something close to a snarl. "Stick around. I'll want to talk to you further." He spun away and followed the officer.

Sylvie groaned. She had really screwed up, throwing what she knew about Perreth into his face. But she couldn't help it. His accusation was ridiculous. How could he possibly think Reed had abused Diana? That Diana had struck back? It would be laughable, even pitiful, if he wasn't in charge of the case. If he wasn't the one who was *supposed* to be figuring out what really happened. The one who was *supposed* to be finding Diana.

Hot tears stung Sylvie's eyes. She obviously couldn't rely on Perreth. Which meant she couldn't rely on the police.

Down the hall, Perreth followed the officer into the lounge. As soon as he rounded the corner, Sylvie started for the church's front door. She needed to find Diana herself. Starting with getting to Diana's apartment before Perreth.

BRYCE WALKER had spent so much of the past week tracking down Diana Gale that when her apartment door opened and an ice-blue eye peered over the security chain, it took all he had to keep from kicking the door in, pinning her to the wall and demanding answers.

"Can I help you?" Her voice carried soft and low tones better suited to a seductress than a murderess. Of course there was no reason she couldn't be both.

"Bryce Walker. I'm an attorney. I need to ask you some questions regarding a case I'm working on." His voice sounded as businesslike and detached as he'd hoped. As if this really was any case. As if he was merely doing his job for a client.

The furthest thing from the truth.

He reached into his pocket, pulled out a business card and slipped it through the narrow opening.

She accepted the card with manicured fingers. "I don't think you want me."

"You are Diana Gale."

"Diana is my sister."

He peered through the small crack, trying to get a better look at her. Blond hair, large blue eyes, a heart-shaped face any man would enjoy seeing on the pillow beside him. A silver eyebrow ring pierced through the elegant arch of one brow, bringing a touch of rebellion to the picture. She held a hand to her chest, spreading pink-polished fingers across cleavage exposed by a formal green gown.

It was Diana Gale, all right. "I've seen your picture. And I know you're an only child."

"I'm Diana's twin. We were separated as toddlers."

She sounded sincere. But then, whatever she said in that musical voice would probably sound sincere. Fortunately he was well aware of his typical male weakness for beautiful women. And he knew how to compensate. "What is your name?"

"Sylvie Hayes."

"And you live in this area?"

"I live in Chicago."

"Where in Chicago?"

"Why do you want to see Diana?"

Normally he might think her abrupt duck of his question evasive. But there was something in her voice. Worry, fear, he didn't know what—but he got the distinct impression she was concerned. About what? His questions? Her sister? Was she really who she claimed? "Are you worried about Diana for some reason?"

"I want to know why you want to see her, that's all. So I can pass along the message."

A lie if he'd ever heard one. And in all the years he'd spent in the courtroom, he'd heard plenty. Not only was he sure she was worried, the prospect that she was telling the truth earlier seemed likely, as well. Maybe she *was* Diana Gale's twin.

Just the kind of woman his brother Ty would have insisted on helping.

A hollow twinge vibrated in his gut like a

plucked guitar string. Bryce cultivated an immunity to beautiful women, but his brother had been another story. Ty would commit the resources of their law firm the moment a tear welled in a feminine litigant's eye.

But then, Ty had been the better man.

"I have a case to discuss with your sister." He peered over Sylvie Hayes's blond head, trying to see into the apartment through the small space in the door. "Will you tell her I'm here?"

"What kind of case?"

"The confidential kind."

"Well, Diana isn't here."

Was she telling the truth? Probably. She didn't seem to be a very accomplished liar. Unlike her sister. "Where can I find Diana?"

"I'm afraid I don't know."

"When will she be back?"

"I don't know that, either. But maybe if you tell me a little more about why you want to talk to her, I can help."

"If you don't know where she is or when she'll be back, I can't see how."

Her lips pressed into a thoughtful line. "You asked if I was worried about her?"

Maybe now they were getting somewhere. "Yes."

"I am. If you tell me what this is about, maybe I can make some sense out of things. For both of us."

Okay. He'd roll the dice. Since the client in this matter was actually himself, the case's confidentiality was as flexible as he needed. "I came across your sister's name yesterday. It was on the sign-in sheet at the Banesbridge prison. She visited an inmate there several times in the past year. I want to know why."

Pale-blue eyes rounded in surprise. Or fear. Or maybe both. "Diana?"

"Yes, Diana."

Her eyebrows pinched together, causing a tiny crease at the top of her slender nose. "I don't understand."

"She signed in as part of a university research project under the supervision of a Vincent Bertram."

"Bertram?"

He did his best to tamp down his frustration. He wanted answers, not to listen to her parrot his every word. "He's a professor in the psychology department."

She shook her head. "Diana is earning her Ph.D. in English. I can't see her finding a lot of twelfth-century poetry in prison. Are you sure it was her?"

"I'm sure." Her signatures on the sign-in sheets were burned on the inside of his eyelids like a brand. "Your sister is the only Diana Gale at the university. The guards recognized her picture. The only other person it could have been is you."

The tiny crease deepened. "That doesn't make any sense."

None of it made sense. Especially not his kid brother's death. "Of course, your sister might have used her affiliation at the university to gain access, and the visit was personal."

"Personal? How?"

"I was hoping you might have some idea."

Once again she shook her head. "I don't." She sounded certain, but her eyes blinked and shifted.

"I would bet a lot of money you do have ideas. Plenty of them."

"I'm sorry." Through the sliver of the opening, he could see her throat move under tender skin. "What prisoner was she visiting?"

He hesitated. The idea of saying the man's name to those delicate eyes already filled with fear felt cruel. And although Ty had accused Bryce of being heartless more than a few times when he'd hesitated to take his brother's charity cases, he was not an abusive man. "My cell phone number is on that card. Have your sister call when she gets home. I'll be up late." He turned away from the door.

Behind him, the door slammed shut followed by the rattle of the security chain. A second later the door flew open and Sylvie Hayes jolted into the hall. "Wait."

He turned to face her.

He could tell she was attractive through the small

space in the door, but he still wasn't prepared for the full stunning view. The green dress flowed over smooth curves like water. Cheeks flushed pink under translucent skin. Wide eyes flashed with light-blue fire and more than a little desperation. "You have to tell me who she visited."

"It's confidential."

"Confidential? I can probably pick up the phone and find out tomorrow."

"Good luck with that." At least *he* wouldn't be the one to break it to her, to see fear swamp her beautiful eyes. He could keep his focus right where it belonged. On the vow he'd made at Ty's grave. On justice.

"Who did she visit? Please."

He should walk the hell away. He should keep things easy, clear. Yet Sylvie Hayes obviously knew more about her sister than she was letting on. Far more.

Down the hall, a neighbor's door creaked open. A young man's spiked red hair poked out. Narrowing his eyes, he watched them with interest.

Bryce spared him a quick glance, then stepped toward Sylvie. "Invite me in."

"Tell me his name."

Bryce shook his head. He didn't need the whole building to hear the inmate's name. Not this inmate. "Invite me in. We'll talk."

She backed into the apartment, pushing the door wide.

He followed her inside and closed the door behind him.

Sylvie stood her ground between the living room and a small dining area. "Okay. Tell me."

"As long as you tell me everything you know about your sister."

She nodded.

"Diana has been visiting Dryden Kane."

He'd thought it impossible for her eyes to grow larger. He'd been wrong.

"The serial killer? The one who hunted women down and gutted them like deer?"

"That's the one."

She covered her lips with trembling fingers. "Are you sure?"

He didn't want to tell her more, but now that she knew, it was only fair. "Your sister visited him once a month, starting seven months ago."

"Seven months? That's a month before I knew her." Her eyebrow ring dipped in a frown. "She never said anything about it. About him."

"You were worried about her. Before I came to the door tonight."

She nodded.

"Why?"

"She was supposed to be married today. But the wedding never took place."

That explained the fancy green dress—a dress,

he now realized, marred with brown smudges. "Is that blood?"

She nodded. "Right before the ceremony, I found Reed—the groom—unconscious and bleeding. Diana was gone."

"You called the police?"

She dropped her hand from her mouth and curled her fingers to fists at her sides. "The police think *she* did it."

In light of what Bryce suspected about Diana Gale, the police were on the right trail. "Do you know for a fact that she didn't?"

She glared at the suggestion as if considering leaving Bryce unconscious and bleeding if he didn't zip it. "Reed is a cop. The detective in charge is out to get him. And now he's out to get Diana, too."

Interesting, though he doubted it was the case. But Sylvie believed it. It had been easy to see through her previous lie. She wasn't lying now. "So why aren't the police here? If they really suspect her, I would think they would be searching her apartment."

"I imagine they're on their way." She glanced down the hall.

"And that's why you're here, isn't it? To search her apartment before they arrive."

She looked down. Her fingers tangled together. Busted. "If there's something that might tell me what happened to Diana, I have to find it."

And he'd like to find it, too. More than she knew. "Then why are we standing around wasting time?"

She stared at him a long moment, as if trying to decide whether she should trust him or not. Finally the press of time seemed to win out. "I thought I'd start in her office."

"Lead the way."

Sylvie marched down the hall, pushed a door open and led him inside.

The office was a neat but obviously well-used workspace. White walls and desk gave the room a clean, fresh feeling. Papers rose in orderly stacked piles. But it was the splashes of color, the artwork and figurines dedicated to female superheroes, that made Bryce's lips twist in an ironic smile.

Too bad Diana herself was no champion of justice.

Sylvie stepped to the desk, sank into the chair and wheeled in front of the file cabinet. She scanned the stack of student papers on top before gripping the handle of the top drawer and yanking it open.

Bryce stepped close behind her, reading the files over her shoulder. Together they skimmed the contents. Student evaluations and files dedicated to her dissertation jammed the first two drawers. Sylvie had thumbed through most of the contents of the third drawer when Bryce noticed an unmarked manila folder peeking from the back. "What about that one?"

Sylvie plucked the unlabeled file folder from the drawer and flipped it open. A photo stared up at them—ice-blue eyes in a face that looked much younger than its years.

The back of Bryce's neck prickled at the sight of his former client's cold, hard eyes.

"Who is this?" Sylvie asked.

"Dryden Kane."

Her shoulders tensed. "I thought he looked familiar. Except that in this picture he looks so normal. Like the boy next door."

Bryce couldn't argue. Dryden Kane *did* look more like an average suburban neighbor than the brutal killer he was. Some might even say he was good-looking. And that was exactly what made him so dangerous to the women he'd charmed into trusting him. God knew Kane's civilized appearance had fooled *him*. He tried to swallow the bitter taste in his mouth. "What else is in the folder?"

She turned the photo face down. Piled behind it were copies of old newspaper articles. Sylvie flipped through the first few, twenty-year-old articles detailing Kane's brutal murders of blond college coeds and his circus of a trial. Behind those were articles half that old telling the story of his prison marriage to the misguided Dixie Madsen and their notorious escape and recapture. More recent articles poked out from underneath in the original newsprint.

Bryce pointed to the photocopies on the top of the stack. "These look like they were made from microfilm."

"Microfilm? Like from a library?"

"Yeah. See how a few of them are in negative? That happens with some machines. And the library is one of the few places she could get her hands on articles this old."

"Why would she copy all these articles?"

Bryce didn't know, but he had his suspicions. Of course, he wasn't about to share them with Sylvie Hayes. "Whatever the reason, she had to be pretty dedicated. It takes a lot of time to go through microfilm."

A piece of paper stuck out from behind the stack of articles: an envelope addressed to Diana Gale, complete with canceled stamp and postmarked last month.

Bryce's heart pounded so hard he could feel each beat in his throat. "Is that a letter?"

Sylvie let the copied article she was reading fall back into the folder and reached for the envelope.

A loud thump sounded from the other room. "Police," a muffled voice shouted from the hall. "Open the door. We have a warrant to search the premises."

Bryce met Sylvie's desperate eyes. They'd barely scratched the surface. He needed to study the folder, to find out exactly what Diana Gale saw fit to collect, what she knew about Kane, and when she knew it. And most of all, he needed to read that letter. If it was from Kane and he had sent it last month, it might give him everything he needed to prove that for whatever reason, Diana Gale had acted as Dryden Kane's conduit to the outside world. And that at Kane's bequest, she had arranged Ty's murder.

Sylvie stuffed the letter back into the folder, snapped the cover shut and thrust up from the chair. "I'm not giving them this folder."

His feelings exactly. But there wasn't much they could do to keep it. Not with the police right outside. "What are you planning to do?"

"I don't know. But I can't just hand this over to Detective Perreth. He'll only use it to twist things, to blame everything on Diana, not to find out what happened to her."

"If the police believe as you say, taking this folder amounts to removing evidence. It's a criminal action."

"I don't care. It might be my only chance to find Diana. To find the truth."

And Bryce's only chance to find out who helped Dryden Kane murder his brother. A chill wound down Bryce's throat and lodged in his gut.

Sylvie ran her hands over her gown. "I was going to change clothes. Why didn't I change clothes?"

There was no room in that dress to smuggle a

folder, that was for damn sure. The chill inside him grew until the walls of his stomach ached from it.

Sylvie dropped her hands to her sides and started for the door. "I'll throw it in my suitcase. I'll say I came to pack my clothes."

"No good. If this Detective Perreth has a brain in his head, he'll ask to search your suitcase before he lets you cross the threshold."

Another thump sounded on the door. The jangle of keys reached them.

Sylvie looked around the room like a trapped animal. "What am I going to do?"

Warmth leached from his veins, chills circulating through his body. He was an officer of the court. He couldn't interfere with a legal search warrant. He couldn't risk his livelihood, his freedom.

He couldn't.

But could he just surrender the folder? Could he give up the only lead he had to nailing his brother's killer before he even got a look?

Oh, hell. "Give it to me."

"What?"

It was crazy. Deluded. Definitely criminal. He watched his hand extend toward her, palm up. As if it was part of someone else's body. As if someone else was taking this leap into the abyss. "Give me the folder."

She handed it to him.

He tossed his briefcase onto the desk, popped the locks and stuffed the folder inside. "Go ahead and pack your clothes. Quickly. I'll answer the door."

Chapter Three

Sylvie jammed jeans, sweaters and toiletries into her suitcase. Her fingers were shaking so badly, she could barely grip the zipper and force it closed. In the other room she could hear the hum of voices. Perreth's blunt rasp followed by Bryce's level baritone. When Bryce had hidden the folder in his briefcase, she'd been shocked. Sure, she'd asked for his help, for an answer to her dilemma, but she hadn't been expecting him to give her either. She certainly hadn't expected him to stick out his neck for her. No one had ever stuck their neck out for her before.

So why had he done it?

He had to have his reasons. But she didn't have time to discover them now. The only thing that mattered right this second was that she and Bryce leave Diana's apartment with that folder. She needed to get a look at the letter, the clippings. She needed some sort of break if she hoped to find her sister. And she needed that break *now*.

She finished closing the zipper, set the suitcase on its wheels and extended the handle. It was time to get out of here and get back to finding Diana.

Before it was too late.

She marched out of the office and down the hall. A small handful of police officers had already fanned out in the living room. Near the center of the room, Detective Perreth glowered at Bryce from under his bushy brows. Sylvie could smell his cologne of stale cigarettes as soon as she entered the room.

"Nice to see you again, Ms. Hayes." He glanced at a uniformed officer who had begun sorting through the drawers in the coffee table. "Thomas?"

"Detective?"

"Take a look through Ms. Hayes's suitcase, will you? We wouldn't want her removing anything other than her personal clothing from the suspect's apartment." He grinned, showing nicotine-yellowed teeth. "It's all right if he takes a look, isn't it?"

"Of course." Giving him an equally phony smile, Sylvie left her suitcase at the mercy of the officer and stepped toward Perreth. "I want to see the warrant."

"I already showed it to your boyfriend here. And the super. It's legal."

Towering next to Perreth's squatty frame, Bryce gave her a confirming nod.

"I asked you to stay at the church," the detective said. "Care to explain why that didn't happen?"

"I had things to do."

"Like what? Rushing to your sister's apartment to remove evidence of premeditation?"

Hot pressure built in her head until it made her ears ring. This whole situation was so stupid. A figment of Perreth's imagination. An attempt to smear Reed and Diana. To get revenge for Reed's reaction to Perreth hitting his wife. And all the while he was wasting his time suspecting Diana, she was in danger. He should be *finding* her, not blaming her.

She gripped the stained satin of her gown in her fists and choked down the words she wanted to spit at him. Making Perreth angry would get her nowhere. She needed to get out of here and find Diana. "I came back to change out of this dress and move my things to a hotel. That's all."

He eyed her gown. "What stopped you?"

"I did." Bryce's voice rippled like waves in water. "We had some things to discuss."

Things to discuss? Sylvie bit the inside of her cheek. Bryce wasn't going to tell Detective Perreth about their conversation, was he? No. That didn't make sense. But why would he want to draw Perreth's attention with a vague claim like that? Surely the detective would want to know more. Maybe enough to detain him for questioning. Or to search his briefcase.

Next to her, the officer finished turning over her clothes and makeup.

Sylvie gestured in his direction. "See, Detective? Nothing. Can we go now?"

"Not so fast." Perreth focused his glare fully on Bryce. Now that Bryce had given him a bone, he obviously didn't intend to give it up so easily. "What was so urgent?"

Bryce shrugged. "Doesn't that go without saying? Sylvie's sister disappeared."

Perreth frowned. He focused on the briefcase in Bryce's hand. "And what do you have in the briefcase?"

Sylvie sucked in a breath and held it.

Bryce offered the detective a bland smile. "Papers."

"Maybe we should take a look at those papers."

The uniformed officer stepped toward Bryce.

Bryce held up a hand. "I'm sorry. I can't let you do that."

Perreth raised bushy brows. "Oh?"

"My briefcase is not listed in your warrant, for one thing."

"Maybe not. But if I suspect you of removing evidence from the scene…"

Bryce shook his head. "As an officer of the court, I can assure you that's not the case."

"You're a lawyer?" The detective pronounced the word as if it were composed of four letters.

Bryce gave him a cool nod. Turning to Sylvie, he cocked his head in the direction of the door.

Letting out the breath she was holding, Sylvie grabbed the handle of her suitcase and took a step toward escape.

"Not so fast," Perreth barked.

She halted. Her pulse pounded so hard it made her feel as if she was wobbling on her feet. Now what?

"Ms. Hayes still hasn't answered my questions. She's coming to the station with me."

No. The hum echoed through Sylvie's head, drowning out the beat of her pulse. She couldn't waste time sitting around the police station answering Perreth's pointless questions. Didn't they say that the first few hours were crucial to locating a missing person? She had to get out of here. She had to find Diana.

Bryce reached into the outside pocket of his briefcase and pulled out a business card. He held it out to Perreth. "Like I said. I'm a lawyer. Sylvie's lawyer. And my client will be happy to talk to you. If you give my secretary a call, she'll set something up."

SAFELY OUTSIDE Diana's building, Sylvie lowered herself into the plush passenger seat of Bryce's BMW. The scent of leather interior with a hint of cologne enveloped her, an atmosphere of luxury and male presence that made her feel as though she'd just stepped into a foreign world.

She'd rather walk.

She wasn't used to people taking care of her, doing her favors, making her indebted to them. She didn't like it. It reminded her too much of the way she'd felt as a child, begging her foster family to take her into their home, wanting so badly to be able to trust them to care about her, and being let down every time.

She strapped on her seat belt and held her satin clutch in both hands. She didn't want to be here, but she didn't have a lot of options, either. Not with Diana's folder still locked in Bryce's briefcase. And although she was grateful to him for helping her get the folder out of Diana's apartment, she didn't intend to take his kindness at face value. She'd learned that lesson before she hit puberty.

After loading her suitcase in the trunk, Bryce circled the car, opened the driver's door and slid behind the wheel. "Comfortable?"

She forced herself not to fidget. "Too comfortable. I'm not exactly used to riding around in BMWs."

A pained smile spread over strong lips. "It's for sale if you want it." He slipped his key into the ignition and the car purred to life. Turning his attention to traffic, he shifted into gear and merged with the flow.

Sylvie eyed his profile in the dimming light. In

all that had happened back at Diana's apartment, she hadn't been very aware of how attractive he was. From short golden-brown hair that held a slight wave to sharp hazel eyes to broad shoulders that looked good in a suit, Bryce Walker was what most women considered a hunk. Add ringless hands that gripped the steering wheel and he became a favorite for most eligible bachelor.

And somehow, that status only made Sylvie more uncomfortable. "Should I give you a retainer or something?"

He kept his focus on the traffic ahead. "Not necessary."

"But you told Perreth you were my lawyer. What if he finds out you're not?"

"You can tell him you fired me."

"Why did you say it in the first place?"

He glanced her way. Puzzlement shrouded his eyes and kicked one side of his mouth into a grin. "He was about to haul you downtown, if you hadn't noticed."

"Of course I noticed. What I can't figure out is why you would care. You don't know me. And you sure don't owe me anything."

He turned his gaze back to the road. "We have the same goal."

"Which is?"

"Finding your sister."

Ah, yes. His case. "Do you lie to the police and smuggle evidence to find witnesses in all your cases?"

"Not hardly."

"So what makes this one so unique?"

A shadow crossed over his face. Evening had crept in while she'd been in Diana's apartment. The car was full of shadows. But from Sylvie's angle, it looked more like a shadow of dark emotion rather than a simple trick of the light.

He flicked on his blinker and took a left turn. "I'm not going to discuss my case with you. But I am willing to help you find your sister."

"And what do you want in return?"

He glanced at her again. "You don't trust easily, do you?"

"I try not to." The truth was, she *had* trusted easily as a child. Too easily. And it had devastated her. Since becoming an adult, she'd learned not to rely on anything or anyone. And she sure wasn't going to forget a lifetime of learning just to trust Bryce Walker—no matter how good-looking and resourceful he was in a pinch. "So what are you after?"

"I want you to share what you know about your sister with me, and I'll help you find her."

She folded her arms over her breasts. "That's it?"

"That's it."

Staring straight ahead through the windshield,

she watched the glare of oncoming headlights. She knew there was more behind his willingness to risk his career and freedom than just to help her. There had to be. Yet somehow that wasn't what concerned her most.

What concerned her most was that she couldn't afford to refuse.

Chapter Four

Bryce pulled an extra chair up to the tiny desk in Sylvie's hotel room and set his briefcase on the dark cherrywood surface. Since he'd made his vow of justice at his brother's grave, every small thing he'd discovered about Ty's death had brought nothing but more questions, more hurdles between him and proving Kane was responsible. Now, for the first time, he had something tangible at his fingertips. Now, he was finally getting somewhere.

He lowered himself into the chair next to Sylvie. Her scent teased at him, flowers with some sort of spicy edge that made him want to inhale more deeply. The jeans and sweater she'd changed into did nothing to diminish her attractiveness. She might look like the photo he had of her sister, yet Sylvie had a freshness in the pink of her cheeks and the light sweep of her lashes that he'd never noticed in another woman. Even her pierced eyebrow suggested the spunky rebellion of a teenager. Yet at the same time she seemed so guarded and distrustful, he couldn't help but wonder why. He couldn't help but want to know more.

Shaking his head, he unlocked the briefcase. He couldn't afford to notice the way she smelled, the way she looked. He couldn't let her contradictions conjure questions in his mind. The last thing he needed was another hurdle between him and winning justice for Ty. He couldn't risk her becoming even a minor distraction. Forcing his attention where it belonged, he dropped the folder on the desk and flipped open the cover.

Dryden Kane stared at them from the five-by-seven photograph.

Sylvie shivered. "Those eyes are so inhuman, so cold. I don't know how Diana could have stood being in the same room with him." She flipped Kane face down on the desk.

As someone who had been in Kane's presence, Bryce couldn't help but wonder the same thing. But there were women who were drawn to serial killers. Titillated by danger, infamy. Why not Diana Gale? Kane had certainly attracted more than his share of female fascination in the past. Hell, years ago he'd convinced a woman to marry him in prison.

Sylvie plucked the envelope from the pile of photocopies and clippings. "It's addressed to Diana. But there's no return address." She slipped the letter out and unfolded it. Reaching to the lamp, she canted the shade to shed more light.

The lamplight slanted toward him, glared off the white paper, making it impossible to decipher the handwriting. But from the abrupt shape of the letters, it appeared to be written by a male hand. He waited for her to read it out loud.

"'You have no idea of the horror I've been through. Weeks of not knowing. Months of asking why. Years of grief. My life is over. Ruined. And he will never pay. Not enough. But you will pay for him.'" Sylvie looked up from the page, eyes stricken. "Oh, my God, Dryden Kane threatened her."

A din of questions swirled in Bryce's head. "Is it signed?"

"No. But it has to be from Kane. Why would she keep it in this folder if it wasn't?"

Maybe it did appear to be from Kane. But why would Kane threaten to make *Diana* pay? And who was she paying *for?*

He blew out a frustrated breath. This hurdle was larger than most. This hurdle threatened to destroy his entire theory of Diana Gale's role in Ty's death. "May I see it?"

Sylvie handed it to him.

It was just a single sheet of typing paper with the words she'd read scrawled across the white surface.

He read it over again to himself. "He will never pay. Who is *he?*"

She lifted one shoulder in a shrug. "Whoever he is, Kane hates him."

"Kane hates a lot of people." Including Bryce. He picked up the envelope and looked at the postmark again just to make sure. Almost exactly a month ago. *After* Ty's death. *After* Kane had sent his message to Bryce by having his younger brother killed.

Pain hit him hard. Ty's death was so fresh, so raw. He shook his head, trying to clear it, to concentrate.

"What is it?"

"Nothing." He handed the paper back to her. Was he wrong about Diana Gale? Was she merely another victim of Kane's charm and brutality? Or had she merely outlived her usefulness? After Ty's death, had she ceased being a conspirator and become a target? And if so, why? "Did your sister give any indication she was being threatened?"

Sylvie frowned, her eyebrow ring dipping low. "She's been upset the last several months. Anxious. I asked her about it, but she blamed it on problems with wedding plans. Do you think she reported Kane's threat?"

"Maybe."

"Perreth didn't say anything."

"Maybe she didn't report it to the police."

"The university."

He nodded.

Sylvie pushed her chair back and shot to her feet. "What was the name of that professor? The one who arranged for her to visit Kane?"

"Vincent Bertram."

She circled the bed. Perching on the mattress edge, she pulled the telephone directory from the bedside table and started flipping pages.

"What are you looking for?"

"A residential listing for Bertram. I'm going to find out why Diana got involved with Dryden Kane in the first place. And whether or not she told him Kane was threatening her."

Bryce tore his gaze from Sylvie and focused on the folder. If Diana Gale had conspired to kill Ty, understanding her motive might be useful. But if she hadn't, he couldn't afford to go off on another tangent.

Eager to see if the folder yielded any more information, he paged through the photocopies chronicling Kane's sordid history. His murder of blond college coeds. His capture twenty years ago at the hands of the FBI. At that point, other than an article here and there, the news coverage skipped about four years to a flurry of stories about Kane's prison marriage and subsequent escape. The stories highlighted the way Kane had focused on his new intended victim, Risa Madsen, a mentor of Vincent Bertram's. The stories continued with the trail of death Kane had left until Professor Madsen and the FBI profiler who'd originally caught Kane had joined forces to subdue him again.

The next articles were more recent, clipped from their original newsprint. The headlines Bryce knew all too well. Headlines he'd *thought* he'd wanted. They blared from the clippings, stinging his eyes. He'd been so stupid, so wrong, so naive. And he'd payed with more than his life. He'd paid with his brother's life.

He sucked in a breath, trying to control the rush of grief, of rage, as he paged through the articles. The stories outlined Kane's lawsuit against the Supermax prison, how attorney Bryce Walker had taken the killer's case, how he'd alleged mistreatment, how he'd won a transfer to another facility. He turned to the last article. A black-and-white picture stared from the newsprint, Ty in the black suit that made him look like an innocent milk-fed farm boy planning to hunt aliens with Tommy Lee Jones.

Bryce's throat closed. He'd been willing to sell his soul to get good press for the law firm, for himself. He'd never guessed Ty's life was part of the deal.

He glanced up at Sylvie. She sat with her back to him, the phone book spread open on her lap. Hunching forward, she copied something on a scrap of paper.

What if her sister didn't have anything to do with Ty's murder? What if she was merely a misguided woman? A woman who never would have been able to worm her way into visiting Kane if he was still housed in the ultrasecurity of the Supermax where he belonged? What if Bryce's representation of Kane had not only led to Ty's death, but indirectly to Diana Gale's abduction, as well?

Weight bore down on his shoulders like a yoke of stone. If he really wanted justice, if he really wanted to set things right, maybe he shouldn't be asking himself if he could afford to help Sylvie Hayes. Maybe he should be asking if he could afford not to.

WITH THE SLIP OF PAPER with Professor Bertram's address stuffed in her jeans pocket, Sylvie crossed the hotel lobby with Bryce by her side and stepped through the revolving door and onto the sidewalk. Saturday night had fully fallen. The neon glow of nearby shops and restaurants and the jangle of people walking down State Street turned the city into a confusion of sights and sounds.

Stepping to the curb, Sylvie glanced at the rush of headlights flowing down the one-way street, searching for a cab. "Thanks for your help. When I find Diana, I'll let her know you want to get in touch with her."

Bryce looked at her as if she were speaking in

tongues. "What are you talking about? I'm going with you."

"Not necessary." All she had to do was to flag down a cab and find the nearest car rental office. Once she had her own car, she'd be able to track down Professor Bertram and hopefully get some answers.

"You need someone to drive."

"That's okay. I need to rent a car anyway."

"Rent a car? Why? I have a car right here." He pointed to his car parked fifty feet away as if she'd forgotten what it looked like.

"Really, I'm used to doing things on my own." It had been disconcerting enough to be forced to rely on Bryce to get out of Diana's apartment with the folder, to drive her to a hotel. Having him in her hotel room, bouncing ideas off him, had only made her feel more jangled.

"How are you planning to find a car rental office? There aren't too many of them around here."

"I'll take a cab."

He arched his brows. "And how are you going to find a cab?"

What, was he playing games with her? "I'll hail one. It's not hard."

"You might find it hard in Madison."

She scanned the street. Not one cab spotted in the flood of personal vehicles. He might have a point. "Okay, I'll ask the hotel to call me one."

"What are you trying to prove, Sylvie? It's been a tough day for you already. You're dead tired and worried about your sister. Driving you around is the least I can do. Besides, you need to find your sister, and I need to talk to her. We have shared goals here."

Of course, he was right about that, too. But even though she could get to Professor Bertram's house faster if she didn't first have to call for a cab and then rent a car, she'd rather have her own wheels. She didn't want to have to rely on Bryce only to have him leave her the moment she needed him most. It would be far easier to rent her own car from the outset than to struggle to pull things together once he cut out on her. "Listen, it's not that I'm not grateful. But I like to do things on my own."

"What, you don't like me?"

"I like you fine." Maybe too much. She doubted she'd ever been around a man this attractive before in her life. A man whose every expression she noticed. A man who made her feel out of control just by looking in her direction.

"You don't trust me?"

He wasn't too far off there. "I don't want to be left in the lurch."

"Why would I do that?"

"In my experience, a more realistic question would be why you wouldn't."

"Listen, you might have had bad luck with people

in the past, but when I give my word, I keep it. No matter what." He gestured to the BMW. "Now are you going to get in, or do you want me to throw you in?"

She shot him a look she hoped conveyed all the annoyance she felt. He wouldn't dare throw her in the car. If he did, he'd get far more than he bargained for, starting with two black eyes.

"Listen, Sylvie, we made a deal. You help me with my case, I help you find your sister."

They had made a deal. A deal she wasn't comfortable with. Not in the least.

He glanced at his watch. "It's already pushing eight. Do you really want to stand around here and argue about this, or do you want to find your sister? It's up to you."

Her heart clutched. Diana had been missing for four hours. Four hours and the clock was ticking. "Okay. For now."

He nodded, as if it was all settled. "Get in the car."

SYLVIE GRIPPED the leather armrest and scanned the beautiful homes scrolling by, trying to spot the house numbers. When she'd first visited Diana in Madison, she remembered thinking the way the downtown funneled into an isthmus between two large lakes was charming. But after more than half an hour with Bryce negotiating hilly, winding one-way streets in the dark, the charm had worn off. "There it is." She pointed to the beautiful stone Tudor lit with artfully arranged spotlights and covered in ivy.

Bryce piloted the car into the home's narrow drive. "Ready?"

As if he had to ask. She was itching to talk to Professor Bertram. To find out what in the world he'd been thinking when he'd arranged for Diana to talk to Kane. And if he'd known about the threats, why hadn't he reported it to the police? Why he hadn't sounded the alarms? But most importantly, she needed to know if he knew anything that could help find her sister.

Sylvie swung her door open and climbed out just as Bryce circled the car. They walked up the cobblestone sidewalk to a front door half shrouded with wide, red-edged leaves of ivy. Bryce stabbed the doorbell button.

Chimes echoed through the house. A moment later footsteps tapped across a wood floor inside and an eye peered through the peephole. "Yes?" A woman's voice.

"My name is Sylvie Hayes and this is Bryce Walker." She projected her voice, hoping the woman could hear her through the door. "We'd like a word with Professor Bertram. Is he home?"

"No."

"Do you know when he will be home?" Bryce asked.

"No."

"Is this Mrs. Bertram?"

Silence.

Strange. Wisconsin Heights was not a neighborhood that seemed to call for a lot of security. Mostly home to university professors and well-to-do business leaders in Madison, it was a safe neighborhood in an area overflowing with safe neighborhoods. Except for the nighttime visit, which would make anyone wary, there didn't seem to be a reason for Mrs. Bertram's apparent paranoia.

Sylvie couldn't help thinking about the night before when Bryce had knocked on the door of Diana's apartment. She had answered, yet had been careful to keep the door chain secured. She'd known at the time that if Bryce had wanted, he could have easily kicked in the door and broken the chain. But even though the chain offered little real protection, after the shock she'd suffered at the church finding Reed injured and Diana gone, she hadn't wanted to expose herself to a stranger.

Judging by Mrs. Bertram's reluctance to open the door, or even to answer, she was even more frightened. Sylvie couldn't help but wonder what or who had spooked her.

Bryce raised his eyebrows at Sylvie. Apparently he had a few questions about Mrs. Bertram, too. "We need to talk to Professor Bertram about a graduate student who is working with him on one of his research projects."

"My sister, Diana Gale," Sylvie added.

"I wouldn't know anything about that. He doesn't live here anymore. He hasn't for many years."

But he'd been listed in the phone book. "You're divorced?"

"That's what I'm saying."

Disappointment seeped into Sylvie's bones like the chill of approaching winter. "Do you have his address?"

"Of course I have it. That doesn't mean I'm going to give it to you."

"We really need to talk to him. My sister has disappeared."

"And you think Vincent can help you?"

"We hope so," Bryce answered.

"What project was your sister working on for Vincent?"

Sylvie hesitated. Not only did she hate saying the name out loud, she doubted dropping Kane's name would do anything to make this obviously frightened woman more open or responsive. But then, not telling her the name wasn't going to get them anywhere, either. "Diana interviewed Dryden Kane."

She could hear Mrs. Bertram's sharp intake of breath even through the door. Silence followed that was so complete Sylvie thought the woman might have walked away.

Suddenly the clack of two dead bolts sliding open cut the quiet. The door inched open and Mrs. Bertram peered out. Skin nearly as white as her hair, she blinked even in the darkness, like a mouse venturing out of a safe, dark hole. "Stop by Vincent's office. He'll be happy to help all he can."

Sylvie let out a heavy breath. "I was really hoping to talk to him before Monday."

The woman glanced at her watch. "He's probably there now."

"On a Saturday night?"

"He usually stops back after dinner, says it's quieter then, better for concentrating on his book. But if your sister's disappearance has something to do with that monster, he won't mind the interruption. He'll do everything he can to help."

Sylvie wished she could shake the woman's hand, something to let her know her appreciation. But despite the way the woman had opened the door to talk to them, Sylvie still got the feeling that a touch from a stranger wouldn't be welcomed. She settled on a smile. "Thank you so much."

The woman gave her a nod and retreated, closing the door behind her.

Sylvie glanced up at Bryce, eager to get his impression of what had happened.

He was looking past her, in the direction of the street.

She followed his line of sight. The one-way street was quiet. Except for an older man walking a dog and a blue service van pulling into a side street, it looked as though the entire neighborhood was spending Saturday night snuggled in their living rooms. "What do you see?"

Cupping her elbow, he steered her down the walk and driveway, toward his BMW. "I'll tell you in the car."

As he circled the car, she jumped into the passenger seat. She had just enough time to secure her seat belt before Bryce pulled away from the curb. "Okay, out with it. What's going on?"

Eyes flitting to the rearview mirror, he slowly wound through the quiet neighborhood and headed west on University Avenue. "Did you notice the van?"

"The blue one?"

He nodded.

"Are you thinking it's strange for a service van to be driving around on a Saturday night?"

"Yes, but that's not all."

"I hate playing guessing games. Will you just tell me?"

"It belongs to a food service. The type of business

that provides produce, meat and canned goods to institutional settings like nursing homes."

That was about as straightforward as another riddle. "Okay, I'll bite. You're wondering what it was doing in that neighborhood?"

He nodded. "On a Saturday night."

Okay, so that did seem odd. But there could be a perfectly innocent explanation. "Maybe the owner of the company lives there. Or an executive."

"Did you see the driver?"

"No."

"Remember the redheaded guy who was listening in on our conversation in the hallway of your sister's building? Diana's neighbor?"

She hadn't paid much attention to him, not enough to pick him out in a crowd. "He's driving the van?"

"It's dark, but yeah, I'm pretty sure it's him."

"Why would he be in this neighborhood?"

"The real question is, why is he following us? Look out the back window."

Sylvie twisted sideways in her seat as if she was talking to Bryce. Covertly she glanced out the back window. Sure enough. Several car lengths back, she saw the hulking shape of a panel van. "You're right. Why on earth would Diana's neighbor be following us?"

Bryce veered right on an exit lane that crossed under the street. "I don't know. But I aim to find out."

Chapter Five

Bryce let up on the gas and watched the distance between them and the van shrink. He didn't want to lose Red. Not yet.

"What are you going to do?" One hand clutching the armrest and the other bracing against the padded dash, Sylvie looked as if she expected him to take off cross-country, four-wheeling it through manicured yards and flower gardens.

There was a day when he might have been arrogant enough to try something like that, just for fun. But *that* Bryce had died along with Ty. "I'm going to set a trap."

He drove several blocks before the narrow road branched off to the left. He flipped on his blinker, making sure their red-haired shadow got a good look before he turned.

"What kind of trap?"

Bryce drove slowly down a road flanked by

forest-shrouded homes. McMansions, really. Status symbols with finished basements. "This drive loops in a circle. Once our guy follows us in, there will be no way for him to drive out without going past us." No need to explain how he knew this, how he used to pass the little jog in the road sheltered by trees every day on the way to the office—the place he now planned to lie in ambush. Driving through this neighborhood was reminder enough of things he wished he could forget.

The road split into two branches, one gliding straight up a hill, one turning sharply into a copse of trees. Bryce chose the hill.

Sylvie twisted in her seat. "He's turning in behind us."

"So far, so good." He kept his speed steady, climbing the hill and driving along the crest. He glanced in the rearview mirror. The panel van was hanging back, waiting until they crested the hill before following. Red didn't want to be seen.

Too late for that.

"What are you going to do once you trap him?"

"Ask him why he's following us."

Up ahead a real estate sign attracted his attention like a rich burgundy beacon. The windows in the mansion behind it were black and as empty as soulless eyes.

Bryce focused on the road ahead and kept driving.

He'd drop the price again if it didn't sell after the open house tomorrow. Hell, he'd give the sucker away. Anything to be rid of it. To be rid of the man he once was. And then he'd junk this car for good measure.

They crested the hill and curved down the other side. Reaching the sharp turn near the creek, he pulled to a stop in the cover of trees. From here they could see both branches of the loop. And anyone following couldn't see the BMW until they were nearly on Bryce's bumper.

Bryce unhitched his seat belt. He had a gun back at his apartment. Good place for it. But unless Red was armed, he shouldn't need it. Not now. He'd had a good enough look at him this afternoon to notice their size differential. Just standing next to the skinny little guy should be enough to intimidate him into talking. He glanced at Sylvie. "Stay here." Opening his door, he climbed out.

He'd wasted his breath. He heard the passenger door open before he rounded the back of the car.

The sound of an engine coasted down the hill and wound toward him. Rounding the corner, the van emerged from the trees. Brakes locked up, rubber screeching against pavement. The driver stared through a bug-spattered windshield, his skin pale even for a redhead. He threw the van into reverse and hit the gas. The engine roared. The van shot backward and slammed into the trunk of a tree.

The sound of steel crumpling made Bryce wince. He'd meant to make an impression, not cause an accident. But the damn kid got what he deserved. Catching up to the van, Bryce yanked open the door.

Red held up his hands as if Bryce were pointing a gun at him. "I didn't do anything. I swear."

At least Red seemed all right. "Why are you following us?"

"Following you? I'm not following you."

Apparently he wasn't so afraid that he was past lying. "And you expect me to believe that?"

Out of the corner of his eye, Red spotted Sylvie step alongside the panel van's snubbed hood. She narrowed her eyes on him. "Who are you?"

"Louis…Louis Ingersoll." He latched on to Sylvie with his gaze. "You're Diana's twin sister. She told me about you."

"What do you know about Diana? Where is she?"

"Diana? That's why I was following you. I hoped you'd know."

Right. As if Bryce believed that one. "Why didn't you just ask if we knew?"

"I was going to."

"Come on out of the van and talk to us for a minute."

The kid looked from Sylvie to Bryce and back

again. "I don't know anything about what happened to Diana. I just know what the minister told everyone in the church. I swear."

Sylvie stepped toward him. "You were at Diana's wedding?"

"Of course. She's my neighbor. I might not have agreed with her marrying that cop, but it doesn't mean I'm not going to show for the wedding if she wants me there."

"You say 'that cop' like you weren't a big fan of Diana getting married," Sylvie noted.

"She was too good for him."

"Why do you say that?" Sylvie asked. "What do you know about Reed?"

"Nothing. Just that he's a cop."

Bryce remembered Detective Perreth's suspicions where Reed was concerned. Suspicions Sylvie had written off as ridiculous, but might be worth checking out. "Did Reed and Diana fight often?"

Even though Bryce kept his focus on Red, he could feel her glare burn a hole just in front of his ear. Great. She'd probably really want to ditch him after this. Good thing she didn't know what he had suspected about her sister originally—before he'd learned about the threat from Dryden Kane. She'd really be upset with him if she knew he'd believed Diana had helped Kane kill his brother.

Red slid out of the van. Hitting the ground, he

shifted one of his Reebok runners in the gravel. "You're thinking the same thing that detective at her apartment was thinking. That he beat her up."

"Did he?"

"If he had, I would have killed him." He balled his hands into fists.

Bryce didn't know McCaskey, but he would have to be pretty small to be overpowered by Red. Posturing aside, Red still hadn't answered his original question. "Did they fight often?"

Red's hands went slack by his side. "I never even heard them argue."

"Did you tell that to the detective?" Sylvie asked in a righteous tone, shooting Bryce a glare.

"He didn't seem to believe me."

So maybe Sylvie was right about her sister and Reed McCaskey. Maybe. Bryce had to admit that whatever the truth was, the longer he was around Sylvie, the more he wanted to believe her vision of her sister. Which unfortunately meant that whoever had abducted her at Kane's orders was probably the same person who'd killed Ty. For Sylvie's sake, he hoped he was wrong. "So why do you think Diana is too good for her fiancé?"

"She just is. Do you know her, man? Have you ever met her?"

"No."

"She isn't just beautiful, she's smart. You know,

like lightning smart." He stared dreamily, as if picturing Diana in front of him now. Only he was staring at Sylvie. "And she has this smile that seems like it's only for you."

Bryce hadn't had much chance to experience Sylvie's smile, but he could imagine what it felt like, way too vividly.

He pulled himself back from that thought. This kid wasn't talking about Sylvie. He was talking about Diana. "So you had some kind of puppy-dog crush on Diana?"

Red lifted his chin, defensive. "She was my neighbor. And my friend."

Now he'd made the guy defiant. A great way to get him to open up. He needed to keep his head straight, remember what he was trying to do, not go off on mental tangents like pondering Sylvie's smile.

Next to him, Sylvie focused on Red, nodding understandingly. "It sounds like you would know everything that went on in her life."

"Not everything."

"Maybe enough to help us find her. To help us save her."

The kid drew himself up. Like any red-blooded guy with a crush, he liked the idea of being a knight in shining armor to Diana Gale's damsel in distress. And with Sylvie asking for his help, too, how could he refuse? "How can I help? What do you need to know?"

Bryce had to hand it to her. He'd cross-examined many witnesses successfully in his day, and this wasn't one of his best performances. But with just a few words, Sylvie had tapped into Louis Ingersoll's vulnerabilities immediately. He stood back and watched, letting her take over.

"You said Reed wasn't good enough for her," she reminded.

"He wasn't. He was there in the room where she disappeared, right? And he didn't protect her. I would have protected her."

"How did you know Reed was there?"

"The detective last night. He told me."

Sylvie frowned.

Bryce knew what she was thinking. Perreth hadn't been overly eager to share information with them. Why would he have confided that detail to Diana's next-door neighbor? A next-door neighbor nursing a serious crush.

The uneasy feeling resumed its creep up Bryce's spine. He could see exactly where this was leading. Thanks to Ty's penchant for helping abused and vulnerable women, he'd seen more than his share of injured male pride and thwarted male desire. This kid had it bad for Diana. And Diana was to marry another man. All the elements for disaster. "You could have done a lot of things for Diana Gale, couldn't you?"

The kid stuck out a freckled chin. "Yeah."

"But she wouldn't let you."

The chin hardened. "Hey, it's not my fault if she was fooled by that whole cop thing."

"You think Reed fooled her? You think that's why she wasn't interested in you?"

"What do you know about it? Diana and me were close. We talked all the time. I knew things she didn't tell anybody else. Not even that cop."

"Like what?"

"You think I'd repeat them to you?"

Sylvie stepped forward and laid her hand on his arm. "Will you tell me? Will you help me find my sister?"

Bryce watched the kid's defiance fall apart like a bad court case. First the chin receded. Then his eyes softened from flint to the consistency of that sweet pink creme inside fancy chocolates.

The unease crept over Bryce's shoulders and wrapped around his neck like a cold hand.

"Did Diana ever mention the name Dryden Kane to you?" Sylvie asked.

"Sure. I used to save clippings for her from the newspaper. She was fascinated with him."

"Did she say why?"

"She didn't need to explain. We have always been on the same wavelength."

"Can you explain it to me?"

"Dryden Kane is powerful, smart…" He shrugged. "A lot of people find serial killers interesting."

Sylvie shook her head as if she couldn't understand the comment and refused to accept it would include her sister. "Do you think he has anything to do with her disappearance?"

"How could he? He's in prison."

"Do you know why he would want to hurt Diana?"

"Why do you think he wants to hurt Diana?" Shaking his head, Red offered her a reassuring smile. "No one would want to hurt her. Everyone loved Diana."

The unease encircling Bryce's throat gave a squeeze. Maybe everyone didn't love Diana, but this kid sure did. To the point of obsession. And judging by the way he was looking at Sylvie, after this little chat, his obsession might just include her, too.

Chapter Six

Fortunately, parking on the university campus was easy to come by on a Saturday night. But amidst the university-wide construction, finding the psych building was another matter. As uneasy as Sylvie felt about Bryce accompanying her, she couldn't help but be grateful; at least he knew Madison. Had she been trying to negotiate the campus alone, she probably would have been walking aimlessly all night. Instead Bryce led her through the maze of buildings with confidence, finally locating the temporary offices serving the psychology department while it appeared the psychology building itself was being torn down and rebuilt utterly from scratch.

It was so quiet in the building, she was surprised to find the door unlocked. A glance at the directory inside the door told them which professors were being housed here and how to find them.

"No Risa Madsen. She must not be at the university anymore."

Bryce tapped the glass covering the directory board. "But Vincent Bertram is here."

They climbed the stairs to the second floor and wound through a narrow hall until they found his office.

The door was closed.

Bryce knocked.

No answer.

Sylvie blew out a frustrated breath. "We must have missed him." She couldn't wait until tomorrow. Since Diana had disappeared this afternoon, alarm had been blaring in Sylvie's ears nonstop. The pinch of it seized the back of her neck. She had to find her sister *now*.

"Are you looking for someone?"

Sylvie whirled toward the quiet voice.

A man only a few inches taller than her, but with the wide shoulders of a bodybuilder, strode down the long hall toward them. His blond hair was liberally sprinkled with white and tapered into almost fully white sideburns that matched his goatee. But the most striking thing about the man was his brown eyes. The dark irises were almost completely surrounded by white, making his gaze very intense. He stared at Sylvie. "Diana?"

She fought the urge to squirm. "I'm her sister, Sylvie."

He strode closer. "Oh, yes, her sister. I didn't know Diana had a twin." He stuck out his hand. "Vincent Bertram."

Sylvie barely contained a relieved sigh. Thank God she didn't have to wait. She shook his hand. His palm engulfed hers, enveloping her hand in a sort of fatherly warmth that contradicted the intensity of his eyes. "I need your help. It's about Diana."

"Of course. Come in." He slipped a key into the lock and pushed the door wide. He gestured Sylvie and Bryce into a small, book-lined room barely bigger than Diana's walk-in closet. The only thing that kept the room from inspiring claustrophobia was the single small window overlooking the lights dotting Bascom Hill. Thankfully, he left the door open.

"I'm sorry for the cramped office. These are our construction digs. They tell me the new psychology building will be beautiful."

Sylvie returned his smile and nodded at the window. "Your view is beautiful."

"That, I'm afraid, won't be quite so nice in the new building. Have a seat, would you?"

Sylvie and Bryce lowered themselves into chairs.

The professor leaned a hip on the edge of his desk and peered down at them. "Now, what can I help you with?"

Sylvie again found herself fighting the need to

squirm. She'd hate to have Bertram as a professor. Sitting under those eyes made her feel as if he could see right through her. "I need to know why my sister's involved in your research."

"The research on Dryden Kane, yes." Seemingly, Professor Bertram had no qualms about saying the killer's name out loud. But then, that kind of comfort probably came with poring over what the man did and said on a regular basis. One grew desensitized.

Sylvie thought of the photo of Kane and all the articles describing what he'd done. Had Diana become desensitized to Kane's evil, too? Did the horror of what he was simply wear off over time?

Sylvie couldn't imagine it.

"Our arrangement is very simple, actually. Diana asked to help, and I took her up on it."

Bryce gave an incredulous grunt. "And you let anyone who asks waltz into a maximum-security prison and chat with a dangerous serial killer?"

"Of course not. Diana was different."

"How?"

"I've done a lot of work studying serial killers, put in a lot of years. Studying Dryden Kane was going to be the crowning jewel of my career. I even talked to a publisher for my book on the subject. Then Kane decided to be difficult."

Bryce leaned forward in his chair. "Difficult? How?"

"He refused to let me interview him further."

"So your book deal was dead." The picture was coming clearer in Sylvie's mind.

"More than that. All the research Risa Madsen had started on Kane and I had continued came to a dead end." He shook his head.

"Enter Diana?" Sylvie said.

"Somehow she'd found out about the work we'd done. She asked if she could be part of the program."

"That still doesn't explain why you let her." Bryce's tone was unmistakably condemning. But though Sylvie found the hints of protectiveness he'd shown her nerve-racking, she warmed to the idea that he might feel protective of Diana, as well.

"Diana said she was going to speak to Kane whether I arranged it or not. So I did. Why not? There was no program without her. No book. Not one of much merit, at any rate. Kane wasn't going to let me interview him. But here comes this intelligent woman who wants to give my work a chance at a second life. And Kane agreed to speak with her."

Sylvie couldn't believe it was that simple. "Didn't it occur to you that you might be putting her in danger?"

"Banesbridge might not be as restrictive as the Supermax, or whatever it's currently called, but it's secure. No one has ever escaped. It's just not possible."

"It would probably be more secure if Kane

wasn't allowed to communicate with anyone who wanted a chat."

Bertram met Bryce's comment with a bland look.

Sylvie shot Bryce a warning glance. Shifting in her chair, she returned her focus to Bertram. "Did Diana report a threatening letter she received from Kane?"

"A letter?" He seemed genuinely surprised. "When?"

"About a month ago," Bryce informed him.

"She didn't mention it." Graying brows hunkered low. "Why don't you ask Diana these questions?"

"Diana has disappeared."

"Disappeared? How?" He raked a hand through his hair, fingers trembling slightly. "Is that why you're here? You think Dryden Kane somehow *caused* her disappearance?"

She wanted to say yes, but the answer seemed ludicrous in the face of the professor's comments about the security at the Banesbridge Correctional Institution. Dryden Kane was an evil man. She had only to look at this photograph, into those eyes, to feel his evil deep in her bones. But he wasn't some sort of supernatural being. He couldn't attack Reed and kidnap Diana from his prison cell. "To tell you the truth, Professor, I came to talk to you because I don't know what to think."

"Have you reported this to the police?"

"Yes."

"Have they found anything?"

"The detective on the case isn't very forthcoming. I don't know what he's found." But she imagined that whatever evidence Perreth discovered, he would use it to prove Diana was at fault.

The professor raked his hair again. "I didn't know. Is there more I can tell you?"

Defeat throbbed through her mind. "I was hoping you knew of something, anything, that could help find her."

He rubbed his forehead, as if struggling to come up with something. "Is there any reason you believe Kane might be involved?"

"Just the threat she received from him."

"The threat?" He shook his head. "She never told me he threatened her. Why wouldn't she have told me?"

"Maybe because she knew you wouldn't allow her to see him anymore?" Bryce offered.

"I wouldn't have. I want you to know that. If I thought she was in any danger at all, I wouldn't have let her near him." He looked to Sylvie. "I'm so sorry, Sylvie. You can't know how sorry I am that any of this had to happen."

She pushed herself up from her chair. "Thank you."

He grasped her hand in his. "The police know their job. I'm sure they'll find her."

At least someone was sure. "If you think of anything at all, will you call me?" Grabbing a pen from the desk, she jotted down the hotel's number.

Bryce and the professor shook hands, and Bryce handed him a business card before following Sylvie out into the hall.

They walked a short distance down the hall without saying a word. For a reason Sylvie couldn't name, she wanted to get out of Professor Bertram's earshot before chewing over all he'd told them—and more importantly, all he hadn't.

Rounding the corner, they nearly ran headlong into a dark-skinned man wearing glasses with the largest lenses Sylvie had ever seen. Behind the glasses, the lines of middle age crinkled around sharp black eyes. "Don't believe Bertram's innocent act."

"What?" Sylvie couldn't have heard him correctly, could she? "Who are you?"

"Sami Yamal. Assistant professor. I couldn't help but overhear. You want to know more? Come." He motioned for them to follow and walked off down the hall.

Couldn't help overhearing? Sure. More likely he was eavesdropping. But Sylvie wasn't about to turn down his offer. She'd take information about Diana anyway she could get it.

Bryce started after the man, Sylvie right beside him. Once they passed the stairs and rounded another corner, Yamal unlocked an office and led them inside. Cubicles and file cabinets jammed a room three times the size of Bertram's office. As soon as they stepped inside, he closed the door behind them. "Your sister was obsessed with Dryden Kane."

Obsessed. Sylvie thought of the file folder Diana kept on the serial killer. As much as she wanted to argue against his charge, she couldn't. "Why do you think that?"

"Things she said. Things she knew."

"Like what?"

He waved a hand, as if brushing the details away like stray crumbs. "Let's just say she did her research before she ever set foot in this department. And that was just the beginning. She wouldn't let it go. She grilled me."

"Why would she grill *you?*" Bryce asked. "Why not go directly to the expert?"

"Expert? You mean Bertram?" He raised his chin, clearly prickly over Bryce's question. "I might not have tenure like Bertram, but *I* was the one who kept the Dryden Kane research going in the years after Risa Madsen left. Diana *did* come to the expert."

"And what did you tell her?"

"I answered her questions."

"And suggested she talk to Kane herself?"

Yamal held up a hand. "I told her not to go near him. Bertram pushed that."

"Bertram?" Sylvie glanced back in the direction of Bertram's office. Had he lied to them? Why? "He said Diana insisted she would visit Kane whether he arranged it or not."

"Diana was eager to know about Kane, no question. But that was it. She never asked to visit him. Until Bertram decided she was the savior of his book deal."

Bryce arched his brows. "So you're saying Bertram pushed her into visiting Kane?"

"Bertram used Diana. And she was happy to let him."

Sylvie nodded. That much Bertram had told them, if not in so many words. "He implied Kane agreed to talk to her because she's a woman."

Yamal let out a short, barking laugh. "Not just any woman."

"What do you mean?"

"Have you ever seen pictures of the women Kane killed?"

The faces from the news articles Diana collected filtered through Sylvie's mind. "Some of them."

Yamal's smile made her want to squirm. He opened a file drawer and pulled a folder. Carrying it to a nearby desk, he removed a stack of photos and spread them across the surface. "One look at these and you'll understand."

A nervous flutter lodged under Sylvie's ribs.

Bryce stepped up beside her. He placed his hand lightly on her arm, as if to guide her to the desk. Or to offer support.

She pulled her arm away. She could make it on her own. Whatever Sami Yamal was about to show her, she'd deal with it as long as it led her closer to finding Diana.

One by one, Yamal spread a variety of shots of smiling blond women across the desktop. "These are Kane's first victims, the ones he killed before he was captured the first time. Notice the similarities? They're all young. They're all blond."

Sylvie didn't have to look hard to see what he was talking about. "And they all look like Diana." And her.

"You betcha." He pulled one of the pictures from the rest and held it in front of Sylvie's nose.

She nearly gasped. The woman in the picture could be her third sister—not identical, but frighteningly close. The style of the woman's blond hair and the puffy sleeves of her jacket dated the picture. No doubt the woman would be quite a bit older than them—if she had lived. "Is that his first victim?"

He shook his head. "His last. Well, until his later prison escape. But she is the most significant of his early victims."

Bryce nodded. "His wife."

"Adrianna Kane. A successful attorney. The theory first developed by Risa Madsen is that Kane had felt controlled by her, a control he couldn't fight against, a control that emasculated him. So he killed women who looked like her to claim back the power he felt she stole." He gestured to the collection of photos with a sweep of his hand. "In effect, he used these other murders to fantasize about torturing, murdering and mutilating his wife. When he finally worked up enough confidence and excitement, he did what he'd aimed to do all along."

She swallowed into a dry throat. "And Diana looks just like her."

"Exactly why Bertram knew Kane would talk to her. And Diana wasn't interested in taking credit for the research or the book. A match made in heaven." Bitterness turned his voice as brittle as a crust of ice. "Diana Gale never should have been put in that situation. She didn't know Kane. She might have hit the microfilm, but she didn't do the years of research required to learn how to handle someone like him. I don't know if Dryden Kane is responsible or not for your sister's disappearance, but if he is, the blame lies squarely with Vincent Bertram."

Chapter Seven

Bryce held the door and ushered Sylvie out of the building. They'd rushed to campus to find some answers; instead, they'd only confirmed their worst fears. That Diana Gale was another victim of Dryden Kane's. A life Bryce's selfish need for publicity had put in danger.

The cool slap of autumn felt refreshing after the stifling heat inside. He sucked in a deep breath and glanced at the vacant slope of Bascom Hill stretching down to library mall and onward to State Street and the glowing white dome of the state capitol.

"Do you really think Kane is behind Diana's kidnapping?"

Bryce glanced at Sylvie's troubled eyes and pale cheeks. She didn't seem like a person who would deny an unsavory fact. Not if it was staring her in the face. But she'd been through a lot in the past few hours. Her desperate fear for her sister must be catching up to her. It was understandable she would look for other explanations to explain what happened to her sister. Other options that weren't so deadly.

Remembering the way she'd pulled away from him when Yamal spread out the pictures, the vehemence with which she'd tried to refuse his help and his car, Bryce fought the urge to touch her, to comfort her. "I'm afraid I do think Kane is responsible."

She shook her head. Apparently he'd given the wrong answer. "It doesn't seem possible. I mean, how could he be? He's in prison."

He'd asked himself the same thing about Ty's death. But in the end, there was no other explanation. In the end there was only Kane's threat and Diana Gale.

"I mean, Sami Yamal seemed pretty bitter," she said. "Maybe he kidnapped Diana. Maybe he wants to use her disappearance to discredit Bertram."

"It seems like there are easier ways for him to do that."

"Or maybe Bertram did it."

"Bertram? She was helping him with his research. He has no reason to want her to disappear."

She blew out a stream of air in frustration. "Maybe she changed her mind about sharing in the book."

"A book that's not written? Not sold?"

"Well, he seems like a more likely candidate than a serial killer who is behind bars."

"You're scared."

She didn't say a word, just started walking faster.

"It's okay to be scared, Sylvie. I'd be worried if you weren't. Kane is a scary guy."

"You hate him, don't you?"

"Of course. I would imagine anyone with a lick of sense would hate Kane."

"True. But with you, it goes deeper than that, doesn't it? That's why you were willing to stick your neck out to get a look at that folder. That's why you're here with me now. You're out for Dryden Kane's blood."

He wasn't sure if he was that transparent or if she was trying to convince herself his real motive had nothing to do with *actually* helping her. "I want to destroy Dryden Kane. But I also don't want something bad to happen to your sister. True. No matter why she was so fascinated with Kane, she doesn't deserve that."

"You think she is one of those women who are attracted to serial killers—a groupie—don't you?"

He wasn't sure why she was asking these things, what she wanted to hear. All he could do was tell her the truth. "Probably."

She dropped her gaze to the leaves scattering under her feet. With her eyes cast down and anxiety digging lines in her smooth complexion, she looked frustrated, hopeless. "I can't believe that about her. It doesn't seem like her at all. But I can't explain why she was so fascinated with him, either."

"Your sister was playing a dangerous game when she entered that prison to interview Dryden Kane."

"But that comes back to what I was saying earlier. He's in prison. Behind bars. How could he hurt her?"

"Just because he can't hurt his victims personally doesn't mean he can't influence someone on the outside."

"Do you really think it's possible he convinced someone to act for him?"

Would he have thought it was possible before Ty's death? Probably not. Did he now? "That's exactly what I think."

She wrapped her arms around her middle and shivered.

Even though he knew her chill was more psychological than physical, he shrugged out of his wool overcoat and draped it around her shoulders.

She held up a hand. "Thank you, but I'm fine."

That stubborn streak again. Stubbornness that only made him want to take care of her more, to help her more. "It's cold. Take it. It's the least I can do."

Grudgingly, she grasped the lapels, pulled the coat around her and continued walking.

"Thank you."

"For what?"

"Accepting my coat. You're saving me from all the guilt I would feel watching you shiver."

"I'm not used to having someone take care of me. Or help me."

"No kidding."

She shot him a frown. The breeze blew a strand of blond against her cheek.

Bryce stared straight down the hill and quickened his pace. He shouldn't even be noticing the way the wind blew her hair. Not if he wanted to avoid driving himself crazy. Not if he wanted to keep his focus where it belonged.

"Who else visited Kane in prison? Besides Diana?"

"No one in the last six months. Just your sister and Kane's attorney."

"If someone is relaying messages for him, acting as a go-between, maybe it's his attorney."

Her idea was so ironic, it took a second for his brain to rattle back into place. "Impossible."

"Why?"

"I know his attorney. Or his *former* attorney, now. The guy's an egotistical bastard, but he'd never be Kane's lackey. Trust me."

"Are you sure there's no one else?"

"There are other possibilities. Too many of them. Prison guards. Other inmates. Any of them could have delivered a message for him."

When they reached the footbridge arching over Park Street, Sylvie stopped and spun to face him. "What if we're looking at this from the wrong angle entirely?"

She'd lost him. He was still recovering from her attorney question. "What do you mean?"

"What if what happened to Diana and Reed didn't have anything to do with Dryden Kane? What if *Reed* was the real target in the attack? What if Diana was only taken to get to him?"

She was grasping at straws again, and the path of her thoughts became as clear as if she'd drawn them on a map. "You're thinking about Perreth."

"He hates Reed. He wants to get back at him. What better way than to attack him and kidnap Diana? God, maybe he can even blame the whole thing on her. That would really tear Reed apart."

Bryce couldn't bear to douse her hope that there was another way out. A way that didn't lead through Dryden Kane. "Maybe."

"You don't think so." She frowned. "Why? Because he's a cop?"

"For starters."

"Cops break the law. Some believe the law doesn't even apply to them."

"Maybe some do. But I haven't met them. And I've dealt with a lot of cops."

"Maybe you've only dealt with good ones.

There are bad people out there, too. And some of them are cops."

"I'm sure you're right. And I agree that Perreth is no gem. But I still think Diana's connection to Dryden Kane is too strong to ignore."

"You're probably right. But I'm not discounting any possibilities." She raised her chin. Her lower lip appeared to quiver slightly, but she caught it between her teeth before he could tell for sure.

The gesture dug into Bryce's chest like a dull and rusty blade. What was he thinking? Dryden Kane wasn't the only possibility. There were others. One came to mind immediately. "You know, of the people we talked to today, I'd be inclined to believe Red is our best bet."

"Louis Ingersoll?" Her brows pulled together. "He *likes* Diana."

"A little too much, don't you think?"

"You think he was stalking her?"

He shrugged. "When she disappeared, she was about to marry another man—a man Ingersoll didn't think was worthy of her."

"And Reed was attacked. Almost killed." She looked up at him with wide eyes. "We need to call Perreth, tell him to meet us at the hospital."

"Why?" Bryce asked, though he had a good idea of where her fears were leading.

"If Louis stalked Diana…if he kidnapped her to

keep her from marrying Reed…if he tried to kill Reed once, he might try it again."

SHE THOUGHT she was prepared to see Reed in the ICU. She'd even told Bryce she could handle it, that he should drop her off and park the car and try to call Perreth at least once more before wrestling with probable cell phone interference within the concrete walls of the hospital. She'd prepared herself while climbing five flights of stairs when she learned two of the three elevators were under repair during the off hours. She'd even had a warning of exactly how hurt he was when one of the nurses manning the nurses' station told her he was still unconscious. She knew she could handle it.

But she was wrong.

At least when she'd found him, he'd looked like himself. Injured, but still Reed, the future brother-in-law she knew. The man Diana loved. Now— swathed in white, with tubes snaking everywhere, his black hair shaved clean, and his face pale and lifeless as wax—he barely looked human. It was as if the Reed she knew had disappeared right along with Diana.

"Can I help you?"

Sylvie spun in the direction of the voice.

A uniformed police officer stood at the curtain

separating Reed's cubicle from the rest of intensive care.

The nurse had told her Perreth had arranged for protection, though she had to see the officer with her own eyes before she believed Perreth had finally done something right. "I'm Reed's sister-in-law. Or at least, I was supposed to be. He and my sister were to be married."

The officer gave her a kind smile. "Do you have identification with you?"

"Yes." She dug in her purse, finally locating her Illinois driver's license. Wincing at the awful picture, she stepped away from Reed's bed and handed it to the officer.

After examining it and checking with the nurses' station, the officer stepped outside the cubicle and pulled a curtain across the open door.

Sylvie moved to the bed. Bryce would arrive any moment. She wondered what he'd think when he saw the officer posted at the door. That she was simply off base about Perreth? Or that she was trying to ditch him again?

She had to admit he'd been a help to her. A big help. And she didn't relish the prospect of running around the campus by herself at night. But the longer he was with her, driving her places, lending her his coat, the more she was beginning to like having him around and the more she knew she couldn't let it go on.

Steering her thoughts away from Bryce and to Reed, she touched a spot of skin on his hand that was IV needle free. She'd heard stories about how people in comas could hear, just not respond. She knew she should talk to him. Say something. But she had no idea what. She had no good news to tell him. And if he really *could* hear her, he didn't need to know the bad.

"Ms. Hayes?" A woman in a white coat pulled the curtain aside and stepped into the room. "I'm Dr. Afton. Mr. McCaskey is under my care."

After some hand shaking and a few pleasantries Sylvie didn't have the patience for, the doctor got down to business. "Our tests indicate we were able to stop the bleeding in his brain," the doctor explained. "I don't expect any long-term problems, but we're still watching him carefully at this point."

"When will he regain consciousness?"

"It's hard to say. Right now the best thing for him to do is to sleep and heal. We'll wait until he wakes up to move him to a private room."

Tears stung Sylvie's eyes. Blinking them away, she reached out and touched Reed's hand. She'd never really thought of Reed as family, but that's what he would be right now if the wedding had gone as planned. God knew, he'd treated her like family. So kind. Protective. He'd gone out of his way to include her and to encourage her and make her feel she belonged, as much as possible, anyway. When Diana had walked into her life, Sylvie had gained not only a sister, but a brother. An actual blood-related family. A family that somewhere deep down she felt she might have a chance of keeping. And she'd thought that someday down the road, after countless family Christmas celebrations and small moments together, she wouldn't feel quite so alone in the world.

Whoever had attacked Reed and taken Diana had almost stolen that possibility from her. From all of them. And if she didn't find Diana, he might succeed in stealing it yet. "Will you call me when he wakes up? I left my number at the nurses' station."

"Of course." The doctor glanced at her watch and stepped toward the cubicle's glass door. "I hope to be talking to you soon."

"Thank you."

A nurse padded in on rubber soles as the doctor slipped out. "Ms. Hayes, we received a call at the nurses' station that you're to meet someone in the lobby."

Bryce? "Oh?"

"He asked if you could meet him just inside the front doors."

"Thanks." Why hadn't Bryce come up? Had Perreth arrived? Were they reluctant to talk in front of Reed?

Heart pounding, she turned back to the bed. "It's going to be okay, Reed. I'll make sure of it."

Taking a deep breath, she stepped out of the cubicle and strode out of the ICU and down the long hall. She hardly glanced at the disabled elevators this time, but headed directly for the stairs.

Bryce wouldn't have asked her to meet him in the lobby if it wasn't important. And if Perreth was the reason he'd asked, she couldn't afford to miss him.

She pulled the steel stairwell door open. The odor of new paint hit her again, just as strong as it had on her trip up. Seemed as though the whole city was undergoing some kind of construction, a frantic last push before winter set in. Of course, they could have waited to paint. At least for her sake.

She started down the stairs. As she reached the bottom of the first flight, a thunk from above echoed off cement walls. Apparently someone else was as impatient as she was, paint smell or no.

She continued down the next flight. Above, the sound of footsteps echoed her own. Perfectly matched. As if whoever had entered the stairwell was doing it on purpose.

Paranoia was setting in big time. Not surprising after all she'd been through in the last few hours, but ridiculous nonetheless. Still…

She slowed her pace.

The footsteps slowed, still matching hers.

Was someone playing games with her? She speeded up, circling the landing.

The footsteps accelerated, too.

Fear pulsed through her. She was in a public building, not some haunted house from a horror flick. Even though it was late, she could open the door on any floor and rejoin civilization. She stopped in her tracks.

Above her, the footfalls stopped.

Her breathing rasped in her ears. Whoever was following had stopped in the middle of the staircase. For no reason other than because she had stopped. "Who's there?"

No answer.

Why didn't he answer? "Is anyone there?"

Her heart thunked against her ribs. She looked back at the door, several steps above. She didn't dare retrace her steps. If she did, he'd hear her. And he could easily intercept her before she could reach the door.

She pressed her fingertips against her forehead. What kind of a person would try to attack someone in a public building? Just a few steps away from help?

Whoever had taken Diana.

She looked down the stairwell. Reaching the next floor was her best bet. Once there, she could find help. Whoever was following wouldn't dare attack her in a hallway bustling with people.

Taking a deep breath, she launched into a run. Her

shoes clattered on concrete. She reached the mid-floor landing. Gripping the handrail, she whipped around the turn and headed down the next staircase.

The thunk of footsteps rang above her. Faster. Keeping time with hers.

She hit the landing and grabbed for the doorknob. She yanked the door open and lunged out of the stairwell.

And into silent, dusty darkness.

Chapter Eight

Sylvie willed her eyes to adjust to the lack of light. In the red glow of the exit sign above the stairwell door, she could see a hallway set up identical to the ICU floor, a short hallway splitting off the main one, the bank of elevators. But that's where the similarities ended. The level she was on was a mess. Giant power tools cluttered the space, each a hulking shape in the darkness. Dust shrouded the industrial tile floor, slick under her shoes. And being Saturday night, there wasn't a soul around.

She was totally alone.

Her throat constricted, making it hard to catch her breath. She had to get off this floor. She had to find people, find Bryce. But the *first* thing she had to do was to hide.

She dashed to one side of the hall, ducking behind one hulking obstacle, then the other. A pallet of tile. An oversize trash bin. When she reached what appeared to be some kind of table saw, she heard the door of the stairwell open.

She crouched behind the saw. She didn't dare move. Didn't dare breathe. She thought she was going to be sick.

The door closed with a thud. Soft footsteps scraped across construction grit.

She tried to peek around the table in front of her. Nothing but more hulking shapes, more red-tinged darkness. He wasn't close enough yet. But judging from his footfalls, he would be soon.

She groped along the dusty floor with one hand. A construction area had to have tools laying about. Didn't it? If she could find something, anything, she could use as a weapon...

Her fingers hit something slick. Plastic. A section of PVC pipe. Not ideal, not anywhere near heavy enough, but it would have to do. She didn't have much to choose from. She wrapped clammy fingers around the pipe.

And waited.

Footsteps scraped closer.

A drop of sweat trickled over her temple. Dust tickled her nose and clogged her lungs. She didn't dare breathe.

The sound of footsteps halted on the other side of the saw. A hulking figure against the red glow. The outline of a man. He was not too tall, but his broad shoulders suggested strength. Much more strength than she could overpower with a piece of plastic pipe.

She listened to his breathing, trying to sense the direction of his gaze. An eternity ticked by. Her lungs screamed for air. Her sinuses burned with the need to sneeze.

With a scrape, he pivoted and moved away. The door to the stairwell opened, then slammed with a bang.

A tremble seized her chest. She sagged forward, against the saw's heavy steel. Slowly she convinced her fingers to release the pipe, setting it quietly on the floor. But other than that, she still didn't dare move. He might still be here. Waiting. She had to be sure.

After a few more minutes she peered over the saw. She could see nothing in the exit sign's light but the tile palettes, sawhorses and other equipment. He was gone.

She straightened. Her legs tingled and stung as blood rushed back into them. Stifling a sneeze, she looked down the hall. There had to be another exit, another stairwell. She didn't dare try the one she'd entered.

Moving away from the red glow, she stumbled through the dark hallway, running her hand along a partially drywalled wall. She rounded the corner and spotted another exit sign, glowing like a beacon. Slipping into the stairwell, she raced down the steps to the lobby level.

The light music of human voices greeted her. She pushed through the door and sprinted to the lobby.

"Where have you been?"

She spun around and spotted Bryce. Worry knit his brow. Worry for her.

She held up her hands in front of her. "I'm fine."

"What happened?"

"Someone followed me. Down the stairs."

He grasped her upper arms. His grip strong, solid. Holding her in front of him, he searched her eyes. "Did you get a look at him?"

"Not really. It was dark, but…"

"But what?"

"It wasn't Louis Ingersoll. The man I saw was bigger. Not as tall as you, but broad. Strong."

"And he chased you?"

She nodded. She didn't want to think about it. The desperate fear. The sudden sense that this was the man who'd taken Diana. "I lost him on a floor that was closed for remodeling." She glanced down at her hands, the knees of her jeans. She hadn't realized until now that she was covered in dust and grit.

"Why didn't you stay in the ICU?"

What? She tilted her head and stared, as if looking

at him from a slightly different angle would enable her to understand. "You called the nurses' station. You told me to meet you down here."

He opened his mouth, a stricken look on his face. "I didn't."

"Then who did?"

"Walker?" a gruff voice said from behind them.

Sylvie and Bryce both jumped. Stepping out of Bryce's grip, Sylvie turned and looked into Detective Perreth's bulldog face.

Bryce stepped toward him. "About time you checked your voice mail."

"Voice mail?"

"I left you half a dozen messages. You didn't get the calls?"

"I haven't had time to check my phone."

"Then why are you here?"

Perreth's eyes shifted to Sylvie. "I need you to come with me."

Bryce stepped between her and Perreth. "For another bullying session like the one you subjected her to earlier? You can't still think she had something to do with her sister's disappearance."

Perreth grunted. "It's not that."

"What *is* it then?" Sylvie's voice rose shrill in her ears. Worry descended heavy on her chest.

"Come with me and we'll discuss it."

"You don't expect her to go with you without

knowing what she's getting into, do you? I won't allow it."

Again Bryce was standing up for her, protecting her. Coming off her experience in the stairwell, she wasn't inclined to tell him to back off. But even though she was scared of what Perreth might say, what he might want, she had to know. "I'll go."

Bryce frowned and gave his head an abrupt shake. "Not until he tells us why."

"Us? There is no 'us.' I'll go."

Perreth's bushy brows hung low. He squared his broad shoulders as if preparing for a fight. "Not here, Walker."

"As her attorney, I can't recommend it."

She opened her mouth, about to remind him he wasn't her attorney, about to demand they leave at once, when Perreth cut her off.

"Fine. Whatever you want." The detective swung his focus to Sylvie. His gaze looked so flat, so dispassionate, it made her shiver. "We need you to identify a body."

Chapter Nine

The trip to the city-county building seemed to take an eternity. Sylvie twisted her hands together in her lap and stared out the window of Detective Perreth's car, willing him to move faster. Every stoplight turned red in front of them. Crowds of revelers decked out in red Wisconsin Badgers gear spilled out of the bars and over the sidewalks, stopping traffic. And even when the street was clear, the cars in front of them never accelerated above a crawl.

Everywhere she looked in the darkness, she could see visions of Dryden Kane's eyes.

Bryce sat next to her in the backseat. She could feel him watching her, his gaze searching her eyes and moving over her face, but he didn't speak. It was as if he sensed she couldn't handle kind words right now. As if he understood nothing could possibly soothe her.

When they finally reached the Madison police's downtown district offices on the first floor of the

City-County building, Perreth led them into a small, cluttered office and gestured to a pair of chairs. "Have a seat."

Sylvie stood. Even the thought of sitting, of allowing her body to be so passive, smacked of giving up. She couldn't believe Diana was dead. The buzz in her ears that had become her constant companion the past few hours was still going strong. The hitch in the back of her neck still pinched like crazy. Wouldn't that have changed if her sister was dead? Wouldn't she feel nothing? "Why did you bring us here? When can I see the body?"

"First things first, Ms. Hayes. Really, why don't you have a seat?"

"I don't want to take a seat. I want to see this body you found."

"Time to quit playing games, Perreth," Bryce said, his voice quiet yet edged in steel. "If you don't at least show Sylvie a photograph right now, we're walking out of here."

Perreth let out a heavy sigh, as if he felt more bored than threatened. "It won't do any good."

"What do you mean? I thought you said you needed me to make an identification."

"I do."

She wasn't following him.

"DNA?" Bryce asked.

Perreth nodded. "We'll take a swab of your cheek."

Sylvie looked from one man to the other. She didn't just want to give a DNA sample. She needed to see the body. If her senses were wrong—the buzz in her ears, the pinch at the back of her neck, the feeling that Diana was still alive—she needed to know. "I have to see the body for myself."

"I'm sorry. That's impossible."

"Impossible? What do you mean?"

"Just that. You're not seeing her."

"Why?" Bryce asked.

Sylvie let out a relieved breath. Despite her need to get away from Bryce, to not let herself to rely on him, she couldn't help feel grateful that he was here now, backing her up.

Perreth grunted. "The body we found was burned. Beyond recognition."

"Dental records?" Bryce prompted.

"Her teeth were removed."

"Removed? Oh, my God!" A sympathetic pain ripped through Sylvie's jaw. What had happened? What kind of horrors had this woman endured before death had finally taken her? "If the body was burned and the teeth are missing, what makes you think it's my sister?"

"Height, build, what's left of the hair—all match your sister. And she's the only missing person we have fitting that description. We need your DNA to be certain."

"But there's a chance it's not her?"

"There's always a chance."

A chance. A hope. No, more than a hope. Sylvie's senses had been telling her Diana was alive all along. The body couldn't be Diana. It couldn't be. "How long will the DNA match take?"

"Our lab will expedite. But the time depends on a number of factors. I can't be any more specific than that."

Specific? He hadn't been specific about anything since she met him. "You'll still look for Diana while you're waiting for the results?"

That bored look again. And no answer.

What little oxygen was in the room seemed to leech away. The scenarios she'd discussed with Bryce on the university campus swirled in her mind. What if Perreth was responsible, after all? What if *he* had killed her sister? Bryce hadn't believed it, and after seeing the guard at the hospital, Sylvie had been inclined to agree. But that didn't necessarily clear the detective. And if Perreth was responsible for Diana's disappearance, he wouldn't have a reason to continue looking for Diana. In fact, he wouldn't want *anyone* looking for her.

She swallowed the accusations she wanted to hurl at him. She didn't have any proof he was involved. Not one shred. And if he was, she didn't want to tip him off that she suspected him. If he wasn't, the last thing she wanted was to alienate him further. Either way, she couldn't let the police call off the search. "You can't stop looking for her. Please."

"Of course we'll keep up the investigation."

"But you're not going to look very hard, are you?"

"We'll continue the investigation, I said. If she's still out there, we'll find her."

She opened her mouth, trying to pull more air into starving lungs. She'd thought Perreth's belief that Diana had attacked Reed and subsequent hunt for her was the worst thing that could happen to her sister. But if the police stopped looking for her entirely… "She isn't dead. She's my twin. I know she's still alive. I feel it."

Perreth glanced at her sideways.

Of course he wouldn't believe she could sense things about her sister. Perreth wouldn't believe her if she told him the earth was round. She turned to Bryce. "She's not dead."

He met her gaze. He *wanted* to believe her. She could see it in the lines of stress fanning out from his eyes, in the pained press of his lips. He reached out and took her hand in his, giving her something to hold on to. "Okay. Then no matter what the police do, we keep looking."

Tears pressed hot against the backs of her eyes and burned through her sinuses. She was so afraid, so very afraid she would never see her sister again. But Bryce was here with her. And though she could tell he feared she was wrong, that deep down he probably believed Diana and the body were the same, he was willing to listen, willing to help, willing to hold on to her—more solid than anything she'd ever known.

IT WAS WELL PAST midnight by the time Bryce walked Sylvie back to her hotel room. He tried to swallow the guilt creeping up his throat. He could never make up for his decision to represent Kane. He could never wash Ty's blood from his hands. And now, if Diana Gale was indeed lying in the morgue, he would have her blood to contend with, too.

He eyed Sylvie as she walked beside him. He couldn't change the past. Couldn't erase what he'd done. All he could do now was to help her get through this, to help her find her sister, provided Diana was still out there somewhere, and bring whoever was responsible to justice.

But they'd done all they could for tonight. Now Sylvie had to rest. To regroup. At least for a few hours. And judging from the way she'd tried to push him away since he'd met her, he doubted she'd let him help her with that. Just as well. He didn't know how much help he could be, anyway. "Do you have someone I could call? Someone to stay with you?"

"No."

"No one?" She had to have someone, didn't she?

Reaching the door, she fumbled in her pocket for the key card. "I'll be fine. Really."

Like hell she would. She might have insisted her sister wasn't dead at the police station, but that didn't mean she wasn't scared out of her mind that it was true—that despite her feelings, the burned, mutilated body in the morgue really was Diana Gale.

She hadn't yet shed a tear, but the dam holding her emotions would crack eventually. When the raw anger and fear finally caught up with her, she was going to need someone to turn to, someone to help her through it.

He had no business being that person. Hell, he'd more than proved he wasn't good at thinking of others. His single-mindedness had been a plus in the world of law, not so in the area of personal relationships. He couldn't count the times he'd let his mother down. And Ty...

He tried to fight past the ache in his gut. The timing now was worse than ever before. Now he wasn't working on a mere case. Now he was working on setting things right, winning justice. For Ty. And maybe now for Diana, as well.

But he couldn't just walk away.

"Would you like me to stay? For a little while at least?" The words were out of his mouth before he realized it, but he couldn't have stopped them anyway. Call it guilt. Call it attraction. Call it sympathy. Whatever had prompted it, he knew it was the right thing to do. The only thing he *could* do.

"I can't ask that."

"You didn't ask. I offered." He waited for her to push him away, as she'd done since they met.

Instead, she dipped her chin. "Thanks." Swiping the key card, she waited until the indicator lights flashed green, then opened the door.

He followed her into the room. It looked the same as it had hours before, but it seemed everything had changed since then. The mood. The heaviness of the air. Him. The last time he'd entered this room, he'd been looking for a way to prove Diana was a murderess. Now he clung to the hope that she wasn't a victim.

He turned to bolt the door. When he turned back, Sylvie was still standing in the center of the room, arms hanging limp by her sides. She glanced around as if unsure where to go, what to do next.

Sylvie had changed, too. A few hours ago she'd been adamant about renting her own car. Now she'd actually taken him up on his offer to stay, to help her through this.

And he'd be damned if he'd let her down. "Sit. I'll get you something to drink."

She sank onto the love seat.

Booze would be good. Just a little to take the edge off. Unfortunately there was no minibar in the room, so he settled for tap water in a plastic cup. He took a seat beside her and handed her the cup. She gripped it with both hands and brought it to her lips. After two swallows, she lowered it. "Thank you."

"Maybe I should run down to a liquor store and pick up some whiskey."

She shook her head absently, as if his words didn't register. "I do have friends. The people I work with at the restaurant, my neighbors, stuff like that. But they are the kind of friends you chat with, maybe drink with after work. That's the kind of friends I have. That's the only kind of friends I really wanted."

"Why?"

She shrugged a shoulder, as if to show it really didn't matter.

But it didn't take a psychiatrist to see how much it did. "Because that kind of friend will never—how did you put it?—leave you in the lurch."

"No," she said. "Everyone will leave you in the lurch sooner or later. With that kind of friend, it just doesn't hurt as much."

"You're kind of young to be that cynical."

"I suppose. But I learned how things work young. I was a foster child, remember?"

He'd forgotten. "Did you live in a lot of different foster homes?"

"Not as many as some kids do." Although her eyes were dry, she brushed them with the back of her hand. "They say you should be grateful for the time you have with someone. But I've never been able to muster that."

They'd been speaking of friends, but he got the idea Sylvie was now thinking of her sister. "I'm not known for being grateful, either."

She searched his eyes.

"I lost my brother recently."

"I'm sorry. I didn't know."

Of course she didn't. She didn't know anything about him. But for some reason, he wanted her to. At that moment he wanted her to know everything. "I had twenty-nine years with my brother. And all I feel is anger that he's gone."

"How did he die?"

"He was murdered."

"Oh, my God."

He needed to tell her the rest. But something stopped him. It seemed cruel to tell her the story of Ty's death just as she was waiting to hear if her sister had suffered the same fate. Probably at the hands of the same man. And if Bryce was being honest with himself, he'd admit that the part of him that agreed to represent Dryden Kane was a part he never wanted her to know, a part he'd set out to eliminate after Ty's death.

"Are your parents still living?"

"My mother is. She lives in a skilled-care facility here in town. But she doesn't really remember Ty, or me. His death never registered." A fact for which he *was* grateful.

"I'm so sorry. Alzheimer's?"

He nodded.

Sylvie slipped a hand over his. Her skin was so warm, so soft.

The ache in his gut spread into his chest. He hadn't talked to anyone but Ty about their mother's illness. How her memories had slipped away, bit by bit, until she hadn't even recognized her sons anymore. "I visit her, even though she doesn't know who I am. I take her for walks, pretend she's still there. She loves looking at the gardens. She's never forgotten her love of flowers."

Sylvie watched him, her expression soft and sad. As if she was absorbing his heartache and making it her own.

As if she needed more. "I don't want to talk about my mother."

"Why not?"

"I stayed to help you."

"You are helping me. Talking is helping me."

He looked at her dubiously.

"I'm sure your mother remembers you. Somewhere deep, I'm sure she senses you're special. I think it's like that with family. I like to think it, anyway."

"You're not so cynical, after all."

She shrugged. "I have my moments."

He smiled. She had more than moments. With just a few words, she'd rekindled his hopes about his mother. They might be only a flicker, but they chased a few of the shadows away. "I don't know. Maybe she does have some idea, however vague. Some days I like to think she might."

"I'm sure of it. Families just get used to taking those feelings for granted. That connection. But that doesn't mean it's not there." She shot him a self-deprecating smile. "The theories of a foster kid who spent too much time longing for something she never had."

So that was what Diana represented to her. That special connection she always wanted to believe in. That she'd never really known.

Bryce let out a pained breath. The prospect that Sylvie might lose her sister after only knowing her a few months crystallized in his bones like ice.

"Ty. That's a nice name."

It sounded nice when she said it. "He was a great guy, for a little brother."

"How much younger was he?"

"Three years. But he might as well have still been a kid collecting strays. I think he lived for pro bono work, representing people who couldn't fight their battles on their own." The ache inside him grew, filling his body and mind until it hurt to breathe. He'd tried so hard *not* to remember how it used to be with Ty, with his mom. He'd focused on everything else—investigating Ty's murder, building a case, plotting revenge—just as he'd focused on the routine with his mom. All so he didn't have to feel this kind of pain. All so he didn't have to acknowledge his guilt. All so he didn't have to recognize he was now alone in the world.

As alone as Sylvie.

He shook his head. "I'm sorry. I didn't stay to relive my own regrets."

"Not all your memories are regrets."

"No." He hadn't realized that, but she was right.

A sad smile wisped across her lips. "You helped me, too."

"I don't see how."

"By showing me it's possible to survive, to go on, even if…" She shook her head. "You know, even if I'm alone again."

He knew he shouldn't touch her, but he couldn't help it. Slipping an arm around her shoulders, he gathered her close. Her body felt warm and delicate. Her hair smelled like spiced flowers. He soaked her in, as if absorbing in her essence would fill that empty place inside him. As if it could blot out all he knew about himself. "You're not alone, Sylvie."

Pivoting toward him, she buried her head in the crook of his neck. Her body trembled against his side and the first trickle of tears seeped into his shirt collar.

Chapter Ten

Sylvie closed her eyes and stepped back, out of Bryce's arms. She shouldn't have let him hold her. She shouldn't have allowed herself to break down, to cry on his shoulder. It didn't matter that his embrace felt so good, so right she wanted to soak it in, to believe for just one moment that she was no longer alone. Letting herself even entertain that possibility was a big mistake. One she knew better than to make.

She ran her fingertips under her eyes, her palms across her cheeks, wiping away the tears. "Thanks for staying. But I'm okay now."

"Are you sure?"

She forced a nod. The truth was, she was far from okay. She was worried about her sister. She was afraid the DNA tests might prove Diana dead. And she'd just cried in a strange man's arms. A man she found impossibly attractive. Impossibly tempting.

She let out a shaky breath. She hated feeling this

way. So out of control, so needy. She was only setting herself up for a fall. And if there was anything she had learned to count on, it was the inevitable fall. "Well, thanks for talking me through this. I think I'll just go to sleep now."

"You're back to getting rid of me again, huh?"

"It's late."

"You're right. I'll see you first thing in the morning."

She shook her head. She couldn't see him again. She'd already grown to count on him too much. Tonight was proof of that. "I've already taken enough of your time."

"You *are* trying to get rid of me again." He tilted his head as if to study her from another angle. "We're supposed to be working together. Remember that part?"

Maybe that's what bothered her. She knew what she hoped to accomplish. But she still had no clue what was in this relationship for him. "Why are you helping me? And don't just give me some line about a confidential case."

He stood, straightening to his full height. "I want to find out who Kane is communicating with on the outside and to put him away. And I want Kane himself back in the Supermax prison. I want him in solitary confinement for the rest of his life."

"Anyone would want that. But not everyone

would smuggle evidence under a police detective's nose or spend their Saturday night escorting a stranger around the city to get it."

"Not everyone has seen firsthand what Kane is capable of."

She nodded. That's how this connected to his case. "You're representing someone Kane hurt?"

He paused, as if debating how much to tell her. "I'm representing the family of one of his victims."

Her stomach hollowed out. Of course. Kane didn't merely hurt people, he destroyed them. Her throat pinched. Again tears pressed at the backs of her eyes. She couldn't go there. She couldn't think of Diana in that way. Her sister was still alive. She had to be. And Sylvie would find some way to make sure she stayed that way.

The ring of the hotel phone cut through her thoughts.

She spun around and stared at the flashing red light. The harsh ring sounded again. Who would be calling in the middle of the night? The lab? No. They wouldn't be able to complete a DNA comparison this quickly. They wouldn't even start the test until morning. Or more likely, Monday.

Bryce took a step toward the phone. "Sylvie?"

It might be about Reed. Or Perreth might have thought of something else. Or Sami Yamal or the professor might be calling with information. She strode to the phone and lifted the receiver to her ear. "Hello?"

"Is this Sylvie Hayes?" A male voice spoke in low tones, barely audible over the line.

She didn't think it was Perreth. But the voice was too quiet to tell for sure. Someone from the hospital? "This is Sylvie."

"I have information about your sister."

"My sister?"

"Are you listening?"

An urgent feeling shifted in her chest. "Yes."

"Good."

There was something strange about the call, the caller. An edginess, maybe. Something she couldn't quite identify. "Who is this?"

"Someone who knows the truth about what happened to Diana Gale."

"The truth?" Cold swept through her, followed by a wave of heat. She pivoted to look at Bryce.

He stepped to her side. Leaning down, he placed his ear close to hers.

She angled the phone so he could hear the caller, too. "Go on."

"Meet me on the bike trail that runs along the Monona Terrace. You know the place?"

She searched Bryce's eyes.

He gave her a nod.

"I know it."

"Good. Be there in a hour and I'll tell you what I know. No police." The line went dead.

Hand shaking, Sylvie lowered the phone. She looked to Bryce, hoping he had heard enough of the call, hoping he knew what it meant. "He said he knew the truth about Diana. He wants me to—"

"I heard." Bryce grasped his cell phone from his belt and started punching numbers.

"Who are you calling?"

"Perreth."

She reached for the phone and stabbed the clear button with a finger. "He said no police."

"Exactly why we should call them."

"What if it's about Perreth? What if he has Diana? I know you don't think that's likely, but he might have more reasons, reasons we don't know about. And if there's even a tiny chance Perreth's behind this, telling him would be exactly the wrong thing to do."

"Did it occur to you that this caller might not want to tell you anything about your sister? That he might be the same person who was following you at the hospital? That he might be looking to grab you like he grabbed Diana?"

It hadn't. She'd only thought about the caller's promise of information. "Okay. You might have a point. But do we need Perreth? Couldn't you come with me?"

"You really thought I'd let you go alone whether Perreth is there or not?"

"No, of course not." She let sarcasm ooze from her voice. "Silly me."

He had the nerve to smile.

"But our little 'deal' aside, if there's any chance he can tell me something, I have to meet him. And I'm not going to let Perreth screw it up."

He stared at her for an eternity. Finally he closed the phone and clipped it to his belt. "Okay, but you need to take some precautions. For starters, your lawyer is going to be armed with more than a law book this time."

BRYCE PLACED A HAND on the cold concrete wall edging the bicycle path and scanned the lights rimming the far shore of Lake Monona. Beside him, Sylvie watched whitecaps crest the rough water and smash against the Monona Terrace's foundation. A stiff October wind buffeted his face and whipped her hair in streaming tendrils. He raised the collar of his overcoat and slipped a hand into a pocket, touching the grip of his SIG-Sauer pistol.

He couldn't quite believe the path his life had taken over the past ten hours. Not only had he broken the law twice—first by removing evidence from Diana Gale's apartment and now by walking around with a gun in his pocket—but tonight with Sylvie something had stirred inside him that he hadn't felt in a long time. He wanted to take his time, examine what that something between them was, what it might lead to. But he didn't see how. Not with Sylvie so worried about her sister. Not when he, too, needed to keep Ty and Diana foremost in his mind.

He took a deep breath, wanting to breathe in her spicy sweet scent instead of just the cold wind.

"Which direction do you think he'll come from? The road?"

"Most likely." Especially if he was looking to grab Sylvie. He'd need a car.

Bryce turned his back to the water and studied the curved white concrete layers of the convention center terrace, parking structure and ground-level parking lot. Even at this hour, an occasional car whizzed past on John Nolen Drive, its headlights illuminating the tunnel under the structure. "He could be watching us from anywhere. On top of the terrace. The parking ramp. Hell, he could even be up in the hotel with a pair of binoculars."

"Or in one of the Dumpsters or loading bays?" She gestured to the service area at the base of the convention center.

"Now you're talking. Name the most places he could be and win a prize." He tried to inject levity into his voice, but the attempt fell flat, his worry winning out.

"What if he thinks you're a cop? Maybe that's why he hasn't shown up yet. Maybe I should have met him alone."

"He knows I'm not a cop. Whoever he is, he knew where you were staying."

"And the only way he could know that is if he was watching me," she finished.

"Right." Bryce had never realized he had a sense for such things, but right this minute he was sure they were being watched. Maybe by Red, maybe by whoever had followed Sylvie into the hospital stairwell, maybe by someone of whom they were totally unaware. But someone was watching them right now. He'd swear to it. "Let's move somewhere a little less exposed. Come on." He brushed her arm with his fingertips, guiding her down the path toward the convention center.

Once they'd slipped into the shelter of the convention center, she folded her arms over her chest. "Will he be able to see us here?"

"No one should be able to see us, that's the point. We were sitting ducks out there."

"If you're trying to frighten me into leaving, it won't work."

"You have good reason to be frightened."

"I didn't say I wasn't frightened. Just that I'm not leaving. Not until I'm certain he's not going to show."

He didn't even try to hide his smile. "You sure are a lot tougher than you look."

"Damn straight. And I always have been. At least, that's what my first foster mother always said."

So she'd been this determined even as a kid. Not surprising. Grit didn't just magically appear when one needed it. You either had it or you didn't. "What inspired her to say that?"

"My heart wasn't fully developed when I was born. Surgery and time took care of the problem, but I was pretty sick for a few years."

"So that's why you ended up in foster care while your sister was adopted."

"There aren't a lot of families who want to take a chance on a toddler with heart problems."

She might have had heart problems as a child, but there was nothing less than fully developed about Sylvie's heart now. Just seeing how devoted she was to a sister she'd known for only six months was proof of that. "Did you have a rough childhood?"

"The families I lived with did right by me. I can't complain."

"But?"

"I guess I just always had the sense that I didn't belong. That they were taking care of me, but they weren't my real family. That it was all temporary, you know?"

He didn't know. But then, how could he? He'd

grown up with his parents hovering over him and his little brother teasing him and breaking his toys. He'd always known he belonged. "Is that where the cynicism comes from?"

"I suppose."

"I'll bet it was hard, moving from family to family."

"Only the first time."

And then she'd gotten used to it? Bryce jammed his hands back into his pockets. "What happened the first time?"

"It's not important."

"You can tell me. God knows I talked your ear off earlier. It's your turn. And besides, if you're going to make me stand out here in the cold in the middle of the night, you're going to have to make it worth my while."

She blew out a breath through tight lips and looked at him as if she didn't believe he really wanted to know.

"If you don't start distracting me, I'm going to have to insist we go back to the car."

"The first couple who took me in wasn't able to have children. I came to stay with them when I was three, and I always remember my foster mother going to doctors and taking fertility drugs, charting her temperature, the whole thing. Finally when I was about eight, she got pregnant."

"So what happened to you?"

"They included me in everything. Watching her belly grow. Shopping for the crib and baby clothes. I even got to pick out these little washcloths shaped like a duckling and an elephant. They fit over your hand like a puppet. I was so excited about giving the baby a bath with those." The smile that had touched her lips while she was reliving the memories faded.

"What happened?"

"The child services people came to get me a couple of weeks before the due date. I never got to see the baby." She shook her head, as if she still couldn't understand it, as if she still felt the sting. "They didn't want to be foster parents anymore. Once they got their real child, they didn't need me. But the thing that kills me to this day is that they didn't tell me. They just called child services. They let me pick out washcloths knowing I'd never get to use them."

"How could someone do that to a kid?" How could they do that to Sylvie?

"Other kids went through worse. Much worse. I was actually very lucky."

Lucky. Right. If having your heart broken as a child was lucky. "Did you find another family?"

"I was bounced around after that. But it didn't hurt. Not like that first time. You learn not to let it."

"How could it not hurt? You were just a kid."

"That's the secret of cynicism. It works a little like a suit of armor." She gave him a dry smile.

A smile that hit him square in the chest.

He couldn't do it. He couldn't stand here and pretend he only wanted to be with her because of some deal they'd made. He wanted to get to know all about her, to soothe her bad memories away, to hold her in his arms and make new ones. He slipped an arm around her.

She looked up at him, searching his eyes.

He wanted to tell her how special she was. How strong and spunky, how warm and sweet. But he couldn't find the words. He'd used words to make cases his entire career, but none would suffice now. He could only show her. He lowered his lips to hers.

BRYCE BRUSHED his mouth over Sylvie's lightly, with more sweetness than passion, more caring than lust, more searching than claiming. But the fire his lips ignited burned to her toes.

She couldn't let herself want this. She couldn't let herself take that step to the edge. Placing her hands against his chest, she pushed him away. "I'm sorry. I can't do this."

His eyes burned into her, fanning the fire. "I'm sorry. I was out of line." But he didn't look as though he thought he was out of line. He looked as though he wanted to kiss her again.

Trembles moved through her like water boiling under her skin. She could say she didn't want to see him, didn't want to be around him, and for God's sake, didn't want to *kiss* him. But she'd be lying on all three counts. And she'd bet he could see straight through those lies. "It's not a good time." He couldn't argue with that.

He nodded as if accepting her answer. "I hope there will be a good time. Someday."

She did, too. But she couldn't tell him that. She could hardly admit it to herself. Not that hope would change anything. No matter what she wanted, no matter what he promised, she knew how things would turn out. And she couldn't let herself take that leap off the cliff when she knew too well how painful it was to land on those jagged rocks below.

"I need some time by myself. It's very late and I'm tired and…" She trailed off. She could see in his eyes that he knew what she was saying. That she didn't need sleep as much as she wanted to escape him.

But this time he didn't argue. He didn't point out their deal. This time he merely nodded and started walking in the direction of the BMW. "I'll drop you off at the hotel."

THE HOTEL PHONE jangled Sylvie from a dead sleep. She bolted upright in bed. Where was she? What time was it? Who could be calling? The details of the day before hit her along with the second ring. Heart pounding, she grabbed the phone in sweat-slicked hands and held it to her ear. "Hello?"

"Ms. Hayes?" A deep voice, calm. Not Bryce. Not Perreth.

"Who is this?"

"Charles Rowe. I'm a resident at the hospital."

Sylvie's heart tripped into double time. "Reed? Is he okay?"

"Mr. McCaskey? Actually, yes. He's asking for you."

"He's awake?"

"He insisted I call. I'm sorry it's so early, but he said it was urgent."

She glanced at the clock: 4:00 a.m. It wasn't even dawn yet. But that didn't matter. Reed was awake. He was going to be okay. And she could talk to him. "Tell him I'll be right there."

"He'll be happy to hear it."

Sylvie didn't wait for goodbyes. She dropped the phone in the cradle, untangled her legs from the sheets and raced into the bathroom.

She ripped off the Chicago Bears T-shirt she'd been sleeping in and slipped on a bra, jeans and a sweater. After brushing her teeth and shoving her feet into a pair of boots, she grabbed her jacket and was out the door.

Outside the hotel, the city was still dark. The streets stretched quiet under the streetlights' glow.

Only an occasional car drove by. She hadn't thought about how she was going to get to the hospital. She glanced back at the hotel lobby. It would take time to call a cab. Time she didn't want to waste.

Of course, she could call Bryce.

She shook her head. As tired as she'd been when he dropped her off at the hotel, she hadn't been able to fall asleep for more than a hour. Instead she'd stared at the ceiling and tried to untangle her feelings. She hadn't succeeded. If anything, she'd felt more tempted to fling herself off the emotional cliff and more afraid he wouldn't be there to catch her if she did.

The roar of an engine saved her from her thoughts. A block away, a Madison Metro bus lumbered toward her. A bus. Perfect. She dashed the few yards to the bus stop.

The bus roared to the curb, brakes hissing. The door opened and she climbed inside, digging in her purse for the fare. "Does this bus stop at the hospital on South Park Street?"

The driver, an older man, squinted at her through wire-rimmed glasses and offered an apologetic smile. "The closest I can get you is about three blocks."

She could walk three blocks. She certainly wasn't going to wait who knew how long for a bus to come along that would take her door to door. "Sounds good." She deposited money in the fare box and took one of the side-facing seats behind the driver.

"It's kind of early to be out and about. Sun's not even up yet," the driver said, closing the door and shifting the bus into gear.

She forced a smile in answer. She didn't want to be rude, but she wasn't in much of a mood for small talk. Her mind was still doing loop-de-loops and she hadn't even had a sip of coffee yet.

"You be careful out there walking. There's been some strange stuff going on. Young women like you getting attacked. Very scary."

Like the body the police found. The body they thought was Diana's.

Sylvie pushed that possibility from her mind. Diana had to be alive. She just had to be. Sylvie wouldn't believe otherwise.

The bus roared down quiet streets. Up ahead the hospital rose over houses and low-riding apartment buildings, dark against the slight pink of dawn just beginning to tinge the sky.

The bus swung to the curb and hissed to a stop. The driver glanced over his shoulder. "This is the closest I can get you."

Sylvie grabbed the nearest chrome pole and stood. "Thanks. I'll be careful." She walked down the stairs and stepped into the cool morning. Holding her breath against a cloud of exhaust as the bus roared away from the curb, she pulled her jacket tightly around her shoulders and started down a block lined with cute little homes surrounded by boxwood hedges.

The lingering glow of a streetlight filtered through orange leaves clinging to the branches of a sugar maple. Her breath puffed in front of her in frosty clouds. Cold poked through her jacket and between the fibers of her sweater, knifing straight to her skin.

She usually loved mornings. The world was so fresh and new at dawn, the air itself feeling ready to burst with potential. But today was different. Whether due to Diana's disappearance, the bus driver's warning or the hush that descended on upper Midwest mornings after most birds flew south for the winter, this morning felt cold, sinister, dangerous.

Jamming gloveless hands into her pockets, she picked up her pace. Three blocks, the driver had said. Three blocks and she could see Reed, tell him all she'd learned, figure out what she should do next.

A car hummed along the street. A car door slammed behind her. The sounds of people. Sounds that should be reassuring but weren't.

She twisted around, trying to see over her shoulder.

A shadow moved between cars and stepped onto the sidewalk behind her. Heavy footfalls echoed, even and brittle, off the dark-windowed houses flanking the street.

Male footfalls.

A dose of adrenaline shot into her bloodstream, setting her already-agitated nerves on edge. The guy was probably returning home from the third shift or after a post-bar-time breakfast. He had every right to use the sidewalk, and she had no reason to feel so panicked. No rational reason.

She walked faster, but still he gained on her. He clearly was in a hurry. Maybe if she allowed him to pass she could push her paranoia aside and focus on what was important—such as how she was going to tell Reed about Diana's apparent fascination with Dryden Kane.

Slowing, she moved to one side of the walk. A thought flashed through her mind, a memory of slowing her steps in the hospital stairwell, of her pursuer slowing, as well.

But his steps behind her didn't slow. If anything, he seemed to walk faster. He drew even with her.

She glanced over her shoulder. Her hair blew in her eyes, obscuring her vision, but she could still make out broad shoulders decked out in a puffy university jacket.

And dark eyes peering out of a red ski mask.

The weather was cold, but not nearly cold enough for a ski mask.

Her heart lurched against her rib cage.

A gloved hand clamped around her bicep.

She spun to the side and pulled back, trying to rip

her arm from his grasp. Her feet skidded. She went down, her knee smacking the concrete.

His fingers tightened, bruising strong. He yanked her to her feet. Her back slammed against a solid chest. His other arm circled her throat.

She pushed out a scream, wild and desperate. She scratched at his arm, his hands, her fingernails scraping slick nylon and leather. She kicked backward, connecting with a shin.

A muffled grunt vibrated through his chest. His arm pressed against her throat, cutting off her voice, cutting off her breath.

Chapter Eleven

A scream vibrated in the dawn air. Sylvie's scream.

Bryce yanked his pistol out of his coat pocket and launched into a dead run. From the moment he'd seen her getting on that bus, he'd had a bad feeling. A desperate feeling. And when the white minivan with no license plates pulled out behind the bus, he'd known she was in danger.

Damn. It had taken him too long to reach his car. Too long to figure out where the bus must have taken her.

Too long.

And to top it off, when he'd reached the hospital, she wasn't there. Not in the drive. Not in the lobby.

And now the scream.

He pushed his legs harder, faster, running in the direction of the sound. His shoes jarred against pavement. Cold air rasped in his throat and ached in his lungs. He rounded the corner onto a side street.

Except for a circle of yellow light from the street-light on the far corner, shadows cloaked this block and the next. But even through the darkness, he could make out the shape of a man a block up ahead—a man dragging something toward a van.

Not something. Someone. *Sylvie.*

She struggled. Hitting. Kicking.

Bryce's heart pounded high in his chest. He pushed his legs to move faster. He had to get closer. He couldn't shoot from here. He'd never hit the guy from this distance. And he couldn't risk hitting Sylvie.

The man stopped beside the van and shifted Sylvie to one arm.

"Hey!" Bryce yelled. "Let her go!"

The man looked in Bryce's direction.

Sylvie yanked herself backward, nearly twisting away. He grabbed her in both arms, pinning one arm to her side. Sylvie fought back, thrashing at the man's face with her free hand.

The muscles in Bryce's legs burned. He had to move faster. He had to reach her before that man wrestled her into the van.

The man pulled back his arm, hand forming a fist. He plowed it into Sylvie's jaw.

Her head snapped back. Her body sagged, dazed and limp.

Rage blistered through Bryce. Adrenaline poured

into his blood and fueled his legs. He dashed across the street and cut through the corner yard, straight for the van. He leaped over a rake lying in the yard and vaulted a low boxwood hedge.

The man slid the van door open. He stuffed Sylvie inside and climbed in himself.

Bryce raised the gun. He was almost there. Almost. He couldn't let the man close the door. He couldn't let him get away.

The door began to slide.

Bryce lunged for it. He gripped the steel edge with his left hand. Fighting to gain leverage, he pulled backward.

The door stopped its slide.

Bryce pulled harder, but it wouldn't move.

A fist shot from the opening, smashing into his nose.

Hot blood gushed down his face and filled his mouth. Dizziness swamped him. He shook his head, trying to clear it. The space narrowed. Steel sandwiched the fingers of his left hand. Pinching. Crushing. He couldn't let go. If the door closed, Sylvie was gone.

He brandished the pistol. "Open the door."

Suddenly the door gave. Bryce slid it wide enough to see inside.

Shadow cloaked the interior, but he could still see a red ski mask, an arm around Sylvie's throat and a knife just under her jaw.

"Back away from the van or she dies."

Bryce released the door. He took a step back and pointed the pistol at the man's head.

"Drop the gun."

Bryce didn't move. If he dropped the pistol, he'd have no way to fight back, no way to keep the man from closing the door and driving the van away with Sylvie inside. "Let her go."

"Drop it!" The man pressed the flat part of the blade against her tender skin. A ribbon of red bloomed along the blade's edge.

A flick of the wrist and she'd be dead.

"Okay, okay." Bryce jerked the barrel up, pointing at the sky.

"Drop it! Now!"

Bryce opened his fingers and let the pistol fall to the ground. It hit the curb and skittered under the van.

The door slid closed.

Bryce lunged for the door. He couldn't just let him take her. He wouldn't.

A thump hit the inside of the door. Then another.

Sylvie?

Bryce gripped the door handle and threw his weight against it.

Something red slammed against the window inside the van. The door slid open like a shot. The attacker's back was to him.

Bryce lunged into the open door. Circling the man's throat with his arm, he yanked him out of the van.

The man swung and missed.

Bryce dragged him back, away from the minivan, away from Sylvie.

The man slugged again, this time connecting.

Bryce's head throbbed. His ears rang. He spun the man around and pushed him over the hedge.

Grabbing Bryce's coat, the man pulled him down with him. They wrestled on the ground, trading punches. The guy was strong. And desperate. Bryce had to find a weapon, something to give him an edge.

The rake. The rake that lay near the hedge.

He groped the grass. His fingers hit the wood handle. Gripping the rake, he brought it up fast. The tines clipped the man under the chin.

A grunt filtered through the mask.

Bryce struck again before the man could recover, this time hitting his side. A sickening thud shuddered up the handle. He could only hope the bastard had a broken rib or two. Share the wealth.

Another swing.

His opponent ducked. And ran.

Movement near the van caught Bryce's eye. *Sylvie*. His heart leaped to his throat. She was right in the man's path to the van. Bryce started after him, but he knew he wasn't close enough. The guy had almost reached her.

She raised her hand, pointing toward the masked man. In her fist she held the gun.

The man dodged to the side. He stumbled toward the van.

Bryce braced himself, waiting for Sylvie to pull the trigger, waiting for the deadly pop of gunfire to split the air.

Nothing happened.

The masked man circled the van and jumped inside. Rubber squealed against pavement and the vehicle roared away down the street.

"Bryce!" Sylvie turned to him. Dropping her arm to her side, she let the gun slide from her hand. It fell to the grass unfired. She hobbled to him, tears streaming down her bruised face. "Are you okay? Please be okay."

"I'm fine. I'm good."

She stopped beside him. Stretching out her hand, she let her fingers hover an inch from his face, afraid to touch. "He hurt you. Oh, God, you're all bloody."

He bet he looked like a mess. He sure hurt like hell. But it didn't matter. All that mattered was that Sylvie was safe. Here. Alive. "Let me get you to the hospital. But I'm afraid we'll be going through the emergency room."

"Sure." She smiled through her tears. "You can take me anywhere you want."

WHEN PERRETH REACHED the hospital, they were still sitting in the ER waiting room. Bryce's whole head throbbed, and the fingers of his left hand were as thick and stiff as bratwurst.

The bruise on Sylvie's face bloomed in a deep shade of pink along her swollen jaw. And her eyes held a glassy look—the result of either a concussion or shock, neither one a nice prospect. But apparently their injuries weren't serious enough to warrant the slightest bit of urgency on the part of the ER staff.

Perreth narrowed his beady eyes on Sylvie and cleared his throat with a wet smoker's cough. "Can you tell me what this guy looked like?"

"He was wearing a red ski mask."

Perreth turned to Bryce. "License plate number?"

"No plates. But he drove a white minivan."

"He's the one who kidnapped my sister. I know it. You've got to find him."

"You're not giving me much to go on."

Sylvie frowned, as if searching her mind for details. "He was about your size and had broad shoulders. And he was wearing a red Wisconsin Badgers jacket."

"Oh, that helps. They're so rare around here."

Bryce fought the urge to punch Perreth right in his sarcastic mouth. "It was dark. What do you expect?"

"What do you expect? Should I go out and arrest everyone who drives a minivan and wears a Badgers jacket? Half the Madison population would be in jail."

He had a point. Their description wouldn't get him very far. But Bryce still didn't appreciate the smart-ass tone. Maybe Sylvie's suspicions were rubbing off on him, but even he was beginning to wonder about Perreth's agenda regarding this case. But then, maybe he was just an ass. "You could start by getting Sylvie some protection."

Sylvie turned to look at him, but she didn't protest. Obviously her need to be on her own didn't apply to all situations. She was a realist when she had to be. Unless she had just been trying to get away from him.

He thought of last night's kiss. Inappropriate. Pure and simple. And it wouldn't happen again. "So, Perreth? Can you arrange for Sylvie's protection?"

The detective looked at him as if he'd just been jolted from a faraway dream. "Police protection?"

"What other kind?"

"Maybe a little common sense? Starting with not wandering around in the dark. Alone. Madison might be a pretty safe town, but there are some bad people out there. Especially lately."

Now a lecture on safety? Perreth was scoring all sorts of points with him this morning. "Sylvie wouldn't have gone out alone without good reason." He turned to her. Waiting to hear it himself.

"I got a call from a doctor. He said Reed was awake and wanted to see me. Have you talked to him yet, Detective?"

Perreth narrowed his eyes on her. "When did you get this call?"

"Right before I left the hotel. Around four this morning."

"And it was a doctor, you say?"

"A resident."

Perreth pulled out a pad and pen. "And this resident, did he give a name?"

"Charles Rowe."

He made another note. "When did you first notice the van?"

"I didn't really. I heard a door slam, and he started following me."

"You're sure you didn't notice him before that?"

Bryce remembered the van that had pulled out of its parking space right after Sylvie climbed aboard the bus. "Why?"

Perreth didn't spare a glance his way. Instead he focused on the door to the emergency room.

Bryce followed his gaze. A nurse emerged from the swinging door and peered at them. "Bryce Walker?"

There wasn't a chance he was letting Perreth get

away without telling him what was going on. Besides, he wasn't sure he even needed a doctor. He'd only come to the ER to convince Sylvie to get checked out. A concussion could be serious, but bruises he could handle. "Take Sylvie."

Sylvie cast him a dour look, as if she didn't appreciate being called away any more than he did.

The nurse looked down at her clipboard. "Sylvie Hayes?"

Sylvie reluctantly lifted herself out of the chair. With one last pointed glance in Bryce's direction, she hobbled to the nurse's side and disappeared through the swinging doors.

Bryce turned back to Perreth. "The van followed Sylvie from the hotel. At least I'm pretty sure it was the same van."

"How do you know that?"

"I was there. Watching out for her."

Perreth frowned. "If you were there, why did you let her go off alone?"

He knew what the detective was thinking, that he'd stayed with Sylvie last night. As much as he wanted to get all self-righteously offended, he couldn't blame Perreth. If he'd had his way last night, he would have stayed.

He rubbed his forehead, trying to forget the torn look in Sylvie's eyes when he'd kissed her, when she'd pushed him away. He shouldn't have done it. The problem was, even knowing it was a mistake, he still wanted to kiss her again. "I wasn't staying with her."

"You were just wandering the hotel?"

Did the detective want him to paint a picture? A pitiful picture of him spending the night in a seating area down the hall from Sylvie's room? Not able to leave her alone, yet certainly not able to stay.

He blew a frustrated breath through tight lips. He had enough of answering Perreth's questions. He needed to ask a few of his own. "Why were you so interested in the call Sylvie got from the resident?"

"I'm just covering all the bases."

"Right. And that's why you wrote down his name?"

Perreth gave him his trademark bored look and didn't answer.

"I suppose I could ask about the guy around the ICU."

"Fine. There is no resident named Rowe caring for Reed McCaskey."

"What do you mean?"

Perreth looked at him as if he were a bit slow on the uptake. "Exactly what I said. There is no Charles Rowe. McCaskey is under protection. Not everyone in a white coat can just waltz in to examine him."

"Is McCaskey awake?"

Perreth didn't answer, but he didn't have to. Bryce could tell from the look on his face Reed hadn't regained consciousness. And it was only a short hop, skip and jump to figure out what that meant. "So you *are* going to give Sylvie police protection, right? Now that you know this guy lured her out of the hotel to kidnap her?"

"I'll see what I can do, but I can't give guarantees."

"Can't give guarantees? Even in this situation? You can't be serious."

He shrugged. "The city budget is serious. We're seriously shorthanded. I said I'll see what I can do."

"What more reason do you need? Her dead body?"

"Listen, if she agrees to stay in her hotel, I can send a uniform over to check on her every couple of hours. But that's as much as I can promise."

"Every couple of *hours?* What's to keep this guy from attacking her between visits?"

He shrugged. "You seem to be around her a lot."

True. But after last night, that had become a problem. A problem, that is, if he was to keep himself from kissing her again. "You want me to do your job for you?"

"Take it or leave it. It's the best I can do."

"The best you can do, my ass." Bryce would love to pummel Perreth's ugly mug, but his fingers were still pretty stiff. "Are you planning to give my gun back? Seems if I'm playing bodyguard, I might need it."

"Don't push it, Walker. You're lucky I just gave you a summons. I could have made things tougher on you."

Perreth must be getting soft. But Bryce couldn't dredge up much gratitude. The prospect of warding off the man who'd attacked Sylvie with nothing but his sore bare hands wasn't a reassuring one. He probably should have kept that damn rake he'd found in the yard.

He looked past the detective, to the swinging door that led to the ER. When it came right down to it, whatever Perreth decided to do didn't matter. Even if the detective came through with police protection, Bryce couldn't walk away now. He had to make sure Sylvie was safe. Letting her down when she needed him most wasn't an option. He would stay with her. He would protect her. And even if he had to tie his hands behind his back, he would keep them off her.

Chapter Twelve

Sylvie looked at Bryce's left hand and winced. Bruises mottled the swollen skin. "Are you sure they're not broken?"

Bryce wiggled his fingers. "See? Not broken."

"How about your nose? That's got to be painful."

Coordinating colors stretched over his puffy nose and darkened the skin under his eyes. "Nothing a few ibuprofen won't fix."

"Didn't they give you anything stronger than that?"

"Didn't need anything stronger." He gave her a reassuring smile.

A smile she could see straight through. "You refused to take anything stronger, didn't you?"

He tilted his head as if studying the bruise adorning his own face. "How about you? Shouldn't they be keeping you here for observation or something?"

She might have a headache sharp enough to split

wood, but she wasn't about to fall for his attempt at distraction. She had the feeling his refusal of medication had more to do with the need for a clear head than lack of pain. "I'm fine. That is, I will be when you tell me what happened with Perreth."

"Or maybe you won't be." Bryce glanced toward the door. "Let's get out of here, go back to the hotel. Perreth agreed to send an officer by to check on you every few hours. I'll tell you what else we talked about when we get there."

"Not until I see Reed."

His lips pinched together in a pale line.

"What's wrong? Is Reed okay?"

"He's still unconscious, Sylvie."

"What do you mean? The doctor called me. He told me…" The tremor inside turned cold. She pulled her jacket tighter around her shoulders and clutched the fabric together at her neck. "The call was a fake?"

Bryce nodded.

"The man who attacked me? It was him?"

"Probably."

Of course it was. Hadn't she thought the call was strange? Why hadn't she put the pieces together? Was she so eager to talk to Reed that she would believe anything without question? "Do you think he's the same man that called last night?"

"Do you?"

She thought of the voice, quiet in the first call, confident in the second, but the same. Definitely the same. She nodded. "So the man who kidnapped Diana is after me."

"It appears so."

"And he's the same man who followed me in the stairwell last night."

"Yes."

"But I've never met Dryden Kane. If he's behind this, why would he be after me?"

"Diana isn't the only one who fits the description of his first victims." Bryce's tone was quiet and matter-of-fact, but the fear running under it was unmistakable.

The same fear that hummed in her ears. She didn't have to search her mind to conjure up the photos Sami Yamal had shown them. The young blond coeds. Kane's blond wife—a woman who looked just like Diana, just like Sylvie. "I'm going to go back to Diana's apartment."

"I thought we agreed to stay at the hotel."

"You and Perreth agreed. I didn't." She started toward the ER exit. "I'm not going to hole up in my hotel room and wait. I need to find Diana, and the only way I can do that is to look."

"Getting kidnapped or killed is not going to help your sister."

"I'll be careful."

"I think Perreth has a point. The hotel is the safest place."

"When did you start listening to Perreth?"

"When he finally said something that made sense."

"It doesn't make sense to me. We only scratched the surface of what we might find in Diana's apartment. What if there's more? More tying her to whoever it is that kidnapped her?"

"Don't you think the police would have found it last night?"

"Perreth was looking for something to prove she and Reed were having problems, that she tried to kill him, for crying out loud. I'm betting there is a lot he didn't think was important."

He frowned, as if he wasn't buying the argument.

"Think about how you'd feel if it was your brother out there instead of my sister."

His expression grew dark, troubled.

She knew it was a low blow, but she needed to make him understand. "I believe Diana's alive. I believe there's something I can do to find her, to save her. You don't have to go with me, if you don't want. But I'm not just going to sit around and wait for her to die."

Bryce grasped her arm, stopping her, turning her to face him. He looked into her eyes with an intensity that made her shiver. "Of course I'm going with you."

Her body warmed. She wanted another kiss. She

wanted to feel that champagne feeling in her blood, that addictive sensation of being hyperalive that she'd only gotten a small taste of last night. She wanted *him*. Great until she really needed him. Great until she threw herself off the cliff and he wasn't there to catch her.

Unable to trust herself to stand here looking at him a moment longer, she pulled her arm away and continued walking. "Great. Where's your car?"

SYLVIE PULLED Diana's key from her pocket and fitted it into the lock. The entire drive from the hospital, she'd been thinking of nothing but Bryce—the way he'd saved her from the man in the ski mask, the way he was here with her and, mostly, the way she felt when she was around him. She couldn't wait to reach Diana's apartment. To focus her mind on finding answers instead of coming up with more questions.

Tumblers aligning, she turned the knob and pushed. The door swung open.

A yelp rang from the kitchen. Louis Ingersoll stared at them, eyes wide.

"What are you doing in here?" Bryce demanded.

"I—Nothing. I mean, I'm watering the plants." He held up a small pink watering can for proof.

"How did you get in here?" Sylvie asked.

"Diana gave me a key. I take care of the place for her when she goes away."

Bryce stepped toward Louis. "She didn't go away, Ingersoll. She was kidnapped. Only yesterday. I'm sure the plants aren't dry already."

"I just wanted to do something for her."

Do something for her? By watering plants that don't need watering? Sylvie had to admit Louis was a little pitiful in his crush on Diana, but this seemed way over the top. "Are you sure you aren't just snooping around?"

Once again, Louis held up the watering can for evidence.

She shook her head. "Why are you really here, Louis? Or would you rather we called the police and you can explain it to them?"

"I swear, I'm not here for any reason. I'm just trying to help. I'm just trying to find her."

Now he was getting closer to the truth. "You're trying to help by looking through her things?"

Louis glanced from her to Bryce and back again. "Well, isn't that why you're here?"

He had them there.

Bryce stepped toward Louis. "There's a big difference. Sylvie is Diana's sister. What are you, Ingersoll? Her stalker?"

"Stalker? You can't think that I did anything to Diana. I would never hurt her."

"That's what all stalkers say."

"I'm not a stalker. I watch out for her. That's all." He looked to Sylvie. "You've got to believe me."

Sylvie watched him. Somehow she *did* believe him. Louis no longer seemed as sweet to her as he had at first, but she couldn't help but feel he was telling the truth. And besides, if the same man that kidnapped Diana was after her, she'd seen him. Not his face, but his body. And he was a little too tall and much too broad-shouldered to be Louis. "If not you, who?"

"Who is stalking her?"

She nodded. "Who kidnapped her?"

"I wish I knew."

Bryce took another step forward. He pulled his cell phone from his belt. "You'd better start thinking before I start dialing."

"There was this guy…"

"Are you making this up just to keep me from calling the police, Louis?"

"No. There was this guy who kept asking her out. He wouldn't leave her alone. She mentioned him once. I think it was someone she worked with at the university."

"Professor Bertram?"

"I don't know his name, but they were working together on the Dryden Kane stuff. The stuff I was helping her with. But I thought he'd finally left her alone when she got engaged to the cop. That's what she told me, when I asked her about him. But then about a week ago…" He shook his head as if troubled.

"A week ago? What happened?"

"It was weird. I didn't know Diana was busy. I went to the door to knock, and I accidently heard him."

More likely he was purposefully eavesdropping. "What did you hear?"

"He was upset. Crying."

Bryce scoffed. "You must have accidently had your ear pressed against the door."

Louis threw up his hands. "He was really loud, like sobbing. I didn't have to try very hard to hear him."

Crying? Could it be the professor? He hadn't mentioned stopping by Diana's apartment, but that didn't mean he hadn't. But why would he be crying? "Are you sure it was the same guy who was asking her out?"

"No. But I know the guy who was crying was from the university. I asked her after he left. She said it was someone she was working with on the Dryden Kane research project."

"And that's all she said?"

"Yeah. She didn't want to talk about it any more than that. Said it was private."

"Why didn't you tell us this before?"

He shrugged, suddenly seeming more self-assured, even smug. "Didn't think of it until now."

"Did you tell this to the police?"

"Like I said, didn't think of it. He's the one who brought up stalking." He nodded at Bryce. "So I got to thinking, maybe that guy was stalking her. Maybe he was sobbing because of her upcoming wedding."

Sylvie brushed the hair back from her face. Was that possible? What if the guy hadn't stopped pursuing Diana when she got engaged? What if Diana had been the one who'd given in? And what if, as her wedding to Reed approached, she'd decided to break off the relationship?

She shook her head. Diana wouldn't see another man behind Reed's back, would she? Her sister had been acting strange before the wedding, and she'd kept her interviews with Dryden Kane secret from Sylvie, but would she really carry on an affair up to a week before her wedding day?

She thought of Mrs. Bertram, her divorce from her husband, the reluctance with which she'd opened the door. Maybe fear wasn't the reason she didn't want to face Sylvie. Maybe the real reason was that Sylvie looked exactly like Diana, the woman who had broken up her marriage.

No. She wouldn't believe it. Not unless she was handed proof. But that didn't mean they shouldn't talk to the professor. Check out Louis's story. She glanced at Bryce.

He lowered his arm and nodded, as if he'd read her mind. "Let's go see Bertram."

AFTER SHOOING LOUIS back to his own apartment, Sylvie and Bryce raced the few blocks to the psychology department's temporary digs. Bertram said he worked every day of the week. She hoped that wasn't an exaggeration.

Sylvie sure hoped Diana hadn't had an affair with the professor. She felt guilty for even considering that her sister would do such a thing, but she couldn't help it. A few days ago, she thought she knew Diana as well as one person ever knows another. Now she couldn't say what was possible.

A weight descending on her chest, Sylvie followed Bryce up the stairs of the old hall. Seeing his determined stride, she couldn't help feeling grateful he was with her. She'd been more guarded with him than she had with Diana, yet he seemed to be proving himself more trustworthy. At least for now.

They reached the top of the stairs and headed down the hall. The air felt different. Colder. They walked past the office where Sami Yamal had shown them the photographs of the women killed by Dryden Kane—the women who looked like Diana and Sylvie. Sylvie peered inside. Two people worked at desks in the large room, but Sami wasn't one of them. She'd like to ask him about Bertram. Get his take on the professor's relationship with Diana. If there was any impropriety at all where the professor was involved, she was sure Sami would have noticed. And with no love lost between him and Bertram, he certainly wouldn't worry about keeping the professor's secrets.

The door to the professor's office was closed, just as it had been the first time they'd visited. But unlike the first time, a light glowed from underneath the door.

Bryce knocked. The door swung open under his knuckles.

Professor Bertram stood in the doorway. Dark circles cupped reddened eyes. Razor stubble sparkled silver over his jaw and shadowed the hollows of his cheeks. A spot of coffee about the size of a half-dollar marred his wrinkled blue shirt.

"Pull an all-nighter?" Bryce said. "I thought only students did that, not professors."

Bertram walked back around the desk and collapsed into his desk chair. "I wish it was as simple as that." He ran a hand over his face and looked at Sylvie. "I'm so sorry."

A tremor of fear shot through her. "For what?"

"Your sister."

Diana? Why would he be sorry about Diana? Her stomach tightened into a knot. "Do you know something? What did you hear?"

"I talked to Detective Perreth. Told him everything I could think of." He shook his head. "It never occurred to me she would be in danger. Kane is in prison. I couldn't have known he had someone on the outside. I couldn't have known I was putting her in that kind of danger. I'm so sorry."

They'd had that theory since seeing the folder at Diana's home office. But Perreth? "Is that what the detective told you?"

"He thinks Diana's disappearance might have something to do with Dryden Kane."

Strange. He hadn't said anything like that to them. He hadn't even given them a clue that he knew about the link between Diana and Kane. "Did he say what made him think that?"

"No. But he seemed pretty sure."

Had Perreth found something? Or had he learned that Kane was Bertram's weakness and he was using the serial killer to get under the professor's skin?

She glanced at Bryce.

As if he sensed her unvoiced question, he pulled out his cell phone along with Perreth's card and punched in the number. Stepping into the doorway of the tiny office, he cupped his hand around the phone and started talking in a low voice to whoever had answered the phone. Judging from his polite tone, Sylvie would bet it wasn't Perreth. Maybe the detective's voice mail.

She turned back to Bertram. He really did look

stressed. Was guilt over getting Diana involved with Kane to blame? Or was what Louis Ingersoll told them the reason? Had he been more involved with Diana than he'd led them to believe? "What was going on between you and Diana?"

His head snapped up. "What do you mean?"

"Diana's neighbor said you were at her apartment about a week ago." Louis hadn't said it was the professor. Not exactly. But after the scenarios Sylvie's imagination had conjured on the trip over, coming right out and accusing Bertram seemed like the fastest way to get answers.

"We were working together. Writing a book. I stopped by her apartment a couple of times."

"He said he heard you crying. Sobbing, actually."

Elbows on the desktop, he cradled his forehead in his palms.

"What were you upset about?"

He let out a shaky breath. When he looked up, tears sparkled in the corners of his eyes. "It's not what you think."

"You have no earthly way to know what I think." *She* didn't even know what she thought. Not anymore. It seemed everything she thought she knew about her sister had been turned on its head. An affair with the professor would just be one more layer of icing on a damn confusing cake. She braced herself. "What is it?"

"It happened many years ago. Probably not very long after you were born."

Not long after she was born? How could his explanation possibly go back that far? She waited for him to continue.

"I had a daughter. Beautiful girl. Brilliant girl. She was only sixteen when she graduated from high school."

Sylvie's mind raced, trying to determine where Bertram was going with this. "What does your daughter have to do with Diana?"

He swallowed hard, as if trying to pull himself back out of his memories, trying to control his emotions. "Nothing."

"I'm asking you about my sister. I need to know about my sister."

"You asked why I was at her apartment. Why I was upset."

"Yes."

"I'm telling you, if you'd stop and listen." Sad no longer, his dark eyes flashed with temper.

"I'm sorry. Go on."

"My daughter was a student here. I was an assistant professor. I was so proud that she chose to come here. I can't even tell you."

Sylvie forced herself to nod politely even though she felt more like wrapping her hands around his throat and strangling the truth out of him.

"She used to have this book group. Just for fun. She and her friends would get together at a restaurant on State Street and talk about the latest releases. One night she never made it home. She was found a week later…murdered by Dryden Kane."

Sylvie gasped.

Bryce stepped up close behind her. She hadn't been aware that he'd finished his phone call. But he was there. As soon as she'd gasped he was there. Before the horror could even take hold.

"That's the real reason I got involved in studying Dryden Kane years later, when Risa Madsen started the program. I had to know why. How he could have done those horrible things to my beautiful little girl. And you know, in all my study, I've never gotten an answer. I never found why." His voice cracked and he buried his head in his hands.

Sylvie let his words sink in. The professor was a victim of Dryden Kane, too. Suddenly his constant work hours made perfect sense. His wife's strange behavior, too. Her fear. Her comment about her husband's obsession fit, too. He'd been obsessed with Kane. So obsessed that he'd shut everything else out of his life, including her. "I'm sorry, I thought—"

"I know what you thought. That I was a horny old professor hung up on a woman less than half my age."

What could she say? That *was* what she'd thought.

That and worse. But somehow the idea of the professor kidnapping Diana because of some obsessive love he felt for her was preferable to the prospect of Dryden Kane being responsible.

"If you're looking for someone who was hung up on your sister, check with my assistant."

"Your assistant?"

"Sami Yamal. I don't think Diana ever actually dated him, but it wasn't for lack of trying on his part. She asked me to have a talk with him a couple of weeks after she started working with us on the project."

"A talk?"

"To suggest that he back off."

Sami? When Louis had told them about the man who'd aggressively pursued dates with Diana and the man who was crying in her apartment, he'd said he couldn't be sure they were the same person. Apparently they weren't.

Heart pumping, Sylvie leaned forward, her palms on the desk. "Is Sami Yamal here today?"

The professor shook his head. "I haven't seen him."

Sylvie's mind raced. Sami was the right size to be her assailant. Had he decided to lay low to hide the bruises she and Bryce must have given him? Or was he with Diana right now?

"Did he call in sick?" Bryce asked.

"Didn't hear from him. But it's Sunday. He

often comes in, but he's not required to be here." Bertram raised a shaking hand to his forehead, as if the hassle of answering their questions was too much for him to handle.

Sylvie felt for the man. He seemed so much weaker than the last time they'd seen him, as if the past hours had taken a horrible toll. Losing his daughter to a serial killer had to be the definition of hell. And revisiting that horror would stress the strongest man. But even if Sami Yamal was the one who had kidnapped Diana and attempted to kidnap Sylvie this morning, even if Diana's disappearance had nothing to do with Kane, she still couldn't excuse the professor for exposing Diana to that evil in the first place. No matter how she could sympathize with his need to understand his horrible loss, she couldn't forgive him. "Where does Sami Yamal live?"

Chapter Thirteen

As soon as they emerged from the building, Sylvie handed Bryce the slip of paper with Yamal's address. Her hand shook. Lines of worry dug into her forehead and flanked her lips.

With the stress she was under, he doubted she needed to be searching down the assistant professor, but he had learned enough about her to know he couldn't sequester her while he tracked Sami Yamal himself. She had to know. And hell, he could hardly blame her for that.

But he could take precautions. "I'm going to call Perreth, have him meet us at Yamal's apartment."

She shot him an uneasy look, then nodded. "I suppose that's a good idea."

Apparently she still wasn't convinced Perreth was on the up-and-up, even though their conversation with Bertram had proven the detective had actually been investigating Diana's disappearance. He just hadn't been keeping them informed about what he knew. "Perreth is a prick, no doubt about it. But he seems to be looking for Diana. He seems to be doing his job."

"I suppose you're right. But I don't trust him."

"You don't trust anybody."

She shot him a crooked smile. "You're doing all right. So far, anyway."

He pulled his cell phone from his pocket and squinted down at the slip of paper to hide the smile beaming through him. He couldn't remember when a heavily qualified half compliment had meant more.

He punched his phone's redial as they walked down Bascom Hill and left the address on Perreth's voice mail. He sure as hell hoped the detective checked his messages. He didn't want to be stuck facing down Yamal with no weapon.

"How far is Sami's apartment?" Sylvie asked when he finished.

"A fifteen-minute walk up State Street, tops."

Sylvie nodded. "What do you think about Bertram?"

"He seems like a man in pain, like all of Kane's victims' families." Like him. Maybe like Sylvie, if her sister was dead.

"Kane did such horrible things. I don't know how those families coped."

Coped? Who said they had coped? Bertram sure

didn't seem to be an example of a family member who'd coped. And Bryce himself sure as hell wasn't. Coping was overrated. He'd much rather get justice. Or maybe even flat-out revenge.

"Sami." She shook her head and increased her pace. "Somehow, I never really considered Sami might be responsible for Diana's disappearance. I know we talked about it, but he just seemed so helpful that day, so proud of his work."

"When Diana and Professor Bertram arranged to work together, they cut him out of the mix. And if he had unrequited feelings for Diana on top of that…" A clear recipe for disaster. Bryce had seen it before, with some of Ty's pro bono clients. Women trying to escape their husband's anger and their love and dependence at the same time. Out-of-control passions always made things more complicated. More volatile.

They crossed the footbridge over Park Street and negotiated their way through the humanities building and down the stairs to Library Mall. The wind kicked up, blowing blond strands across Sylvie's face; she brushed them out of the way. "Diana getting the job of interviewing Kane had to kill him."

"Maybe. Or maybe he found another way of communicating with Kane."

"You mean, maybe he's doing all this for Kane? Kidnapping Diana? Attacking me?"

"It's possible. He could be using another inmate as a conduit. Or a prison guard. Think about it. Yamal is certainly as obsessed with Kane as Bertram is. He has spent his life studying the monster. Whether you're talking about Yamal's obsession with Diana or his obsession with Kane, he's a good candidate for kidnapping your sister." And for killing Ty. "Exactly the reason I think Perreth should be there."

"I hope he gets there before I do. If Sami Yamal hurt Diana, I might just kill him with my bare hands." Sylvie set her chin and marched straight ahead.

Bryce was sure she meant every word. He could imagine her hands around Yamal's throat, choking the life out of him. But he recognized the vulnerability under her bravado, too. The fear for her sister. Her brave facade was as transparent as glass. And as fragile.

Bryce fought the urge to touch her. There was definitely something growing between them. Something he wanted to tend, to encourage to blossom. But it needed time to take root. Time and attention neither one of them could spare. Not right now. And rushing was too risky. He'd learned that when he'd kissed her last night. Rushing could destroy whatever tender shoots he'd established.

Emerging from Library Mall, they crossed Lake Street and started up State in the direction of the capitol dome. Several blocks up, they turned off State Street and located the old Victorian home at the address Bertram had given them. The house had been separated into three flats, each with a separate entrance.

Sylvie poked the buzzer next to Yamal's name. No answer.

Bryce cupped a sore hand and shielded the window in the door. Through the wavy old glass, he could see a staircase stretching to the second floor. Just looking at the stairs, Bryce could see Yamal didn't believe in cleanliness. Tiny muddy cat tracks peppered the old linoleum. And at the base of the stairs, a small orange feline peered at the window and mewed incessantly. "His cat is home."

Sylvie pressed up next to Bryce and peered in. "She seems upset. Do you think something's wrong and she's trying to let us know?"

"Do cats do that?"

"Not a cat person?"

"Not a pet person. I like animals, but I don't have enough time to do them justice. I don't even have house plants." God, he sounded pitiful. Lonely.

"One of my foster families had a cat. Believe me, when anything was wrong, she'd let you know."

The cat paced back and forth on the stairs without taking its eyes from their faces. Its meow was low, urgent.

Sylvie put a hand on the doorknob and twisted. It turned under her fingers. "My God, it's open."

A trickle of foreboding ran down Bryce's spine. "Perreth should be here any minute."

Ignoring him, Sylvie pushed the door inward. She stepped inside, stopping at the base of the stairs as the cat wrapped itself around her legs. She bent to stroke the animal's arching back.

The scent hit Bryce through the open door. Blood. Death. Memories of finding Ty flooded his mind and turned his stomach. The smell. The blood. The gut-churning grief. "Sylvie. Get out of there."

She turned to him, wide-eyed. "That smell. Is it—"

"Wait for the police."

She turned back to the steps. "I have to know."

He grabbed her arm before she could start up the staircase. He couldn't let her see whatever caused that smell. Damn, he wished he had his pistol. Except for his cell phone, he was empty-handed.

"I can't just stand here, Bryce. I have to know." Sylvie tried to pull her arm away.

He held on. Where was Perreth?

"Please, Bryce. If that body in the morgue isn't Diana…"

Maybe the body upstairs was? "Don't think that way."

"I can't help it. Imagine how you would feel."

He didn't have to imagine. He'd smelled the sickly sweet odor of death as soon as he'd opened Ty's front door. Even though he'd never smelled human blood, human death, before that time, he'd known what the scent was, what it meant. It hadn't stopped him. It hadn't even slowed him down. "Okay, stay behind me."

He slipped his hand down her arm until he gripped her palm in his. Holding her hand, he started up the stairs, stepping on the edge of the linoleum to avoid walking on the cat tracks—tracks of blood, not mud. "We can't touch anything. This is a crime scene. We can't destroy evidence that might help the police."

Sylvie crept behind him. Her hand trembled in his, but her steps were steady. From the bottom of the stairs, the cat's mewing grew louder, the sound emanating from deep in its throat.

They approached the dark doorway at the top of the stairs. Bryce's eyes drew even with the floor above. More tracks spotted the wood. The smell clogged his throat. Memories crashed through his mind. Ty's broken body lying twisted on the edge of his bed. The puddle of blood soaking the sheets and dripping into the carpet.

Placing a hand on the door frame, Bryce steadied himself and peered into the apartment. Blood spread over the hardwood floor, not fresh, but brown and sticky. And just inside the archway leading to the kitchen, Sami Yamal stared at them through shattered lenses. A ravaged hole gaped where the top of his skull should be. And in his hand, he still held his gun.

SYLVIE STARED at her reflection in the bathroom mirror. Hair tousled and wet and body wrapped in a towel, she looked tired. Shell-shocked. No surprise there. As hard as she tried, she couldn't erase images of Sami Yamal's apparent suicide from her mind. The blood on the floor. The dead stare of his eyes. The smell that had filled her nostrils, clung to her hair and permeated her clothes.

After she and Bryce had answered Perreth's questions for what seemed like hours, Bryce drove her to the hotel and insisted on accompanying her to her room. She should have objected. When he'd paused in the hallway, waiting for an invitation inside, she should have simply closed the door. But after what she'd seen at Sami's apartment, she couldn't bring herself to shut him out.

She listened to the rhythm of his footsteps as he paced the floor outside the bathroom door. She couldn't imagine what she would have done if she'd come across Sami's body by herself. Even now, the horror of it hung on the edges of her mind, as strong and hard to get rid of as the memory of that smell.

She leaned on the vanity, trying to catch her breath. A sob worked up her throat and echoed in the bathroom. She could never forget how she'd felt walking into that apartment, smelling that odor and thinking in the back of her mind that it could be Diana. That her sister really might be dead.

A knock on the door. "Sylvie? Are you okay?"

Her knees trembled. She grasped the towel, pulling the terry cloth tighter around her body. "I'm fine." Her voice broke. She closed her eyes.

"Open the door."

She fought the confusion bubbling in her blood, the temptation to lean on a man she hardly knew. A man who might be gone tomorrow. She had to pull herself together. She couldn't let him stand out there. She couldn't hide in here and make him worry she was falling apart. "Just a second."

She let the towel fall to the floor and pulled on her robe. Tying the sash securely, she took a deep breath and turned to the door. Pulling it open, she peered out at him. "See? I'm okay."

Forehead lined with concern, he searched her eyes. "Sure?"

Barely above a whisper, his one word carried so much concern—concern for her—tears came to her eyes.

"I thought so." He stepped into the bathroom, behind her. Meeting her gaze in the mirror, he lay a warm hand lightly on the sleeve of her robe. "You've never seen a dead body before, have you?"

She shook her head. She should have known better than to believe she could hide what she was feeling. They might not have known each other very long, but the events of the past few days had convinced her that at times he knew what she was feeling before she did. "I keep seeing his eyes. Those staring, empty eyes."

"Don't think about it."

"I can't help it." A sob hiccupped in her throat. "I keep seeing Diana."

He wrapped his arms around her. His chest and the firm plane of his stomach pressed against her back.

The press of his body felt so good, so right. Just what she wanted. Just what she needed. Just what she couldn't have.

She tried to step forward, to move away from him, but the vanity blocked her. "I can't do this."

He let out a long breath. Slipping his hand along her cheek, he brushed her hair back from her face, draping it over her shoulder. "Let me just hold you. Let me wipe those images from your mind." His breath whispered against her neck.

A shiver rippled over her skin. Not a shiver of cold, though. A shiver of anticipation. She wanted him to hold her. She wanted much more. But… "You might be gone tomorrow."

"I won't be. I'll be right here."

"That's worse."

He met her eyes in the mirror. His eyebrows dipped low with confusion, with questions.

He deserved an explanation. As much as she didn't want to voice her fears, her insecurities, he deserved to know where he stood. "The longer you're here, the more I'll rely on you. The more I'll…" Her voice faltered. The more she'd what?

"You're still worried I'll leave you in the lurch. That just when you need me, I won't be there."

She nodded.

"It doesn't have to be that way. Not with us."

"I wish I could believe that." She'd give almost anything to believe it, for it to be true.

"I wish you could trust me."

She swallowed into an aching throat. "I do trust you on some level. I just…"

"Can't go that far?"

"No. It hurts too much."

"I don't want you to hurt, Sylvie. You shouldn't ever have to hurt." He hugged her tighter, fitting her back tight against his chest. "Just let me hold you. That's all. It doesn't have to go further than that. Just let me take care of you tonight."

His offer sounded good. It sounded wonderful. The trouble was, if she gave in, if she opened herself to temptation, *she* would be the one who wanted it to go further. *She* would be the one who needed more. "I know I sound like such a coward. I sound so weak. I guess I am."

"You?" A laugh rumbled in his chest. "You're the bravest, strongest woman I've ever known."

The warmth of his laugh, his words, reverberated through her back and wrapped around her heart. He made her feel so warm, so wanted. As though she'd finally found her place in the world. A place where she, and only she, belonged. A place she might even be able to pretend was permanent.

At least for one night.

She turned in his arms. Tilting her head back, she looked up at him. She needed to feel those things. Needed what he could give her. If he was gone tomorrow or next week or next month, so be it. She needed him now.

Locking her arms around his neck, she pulled him down to her.

He fitted his mouth over hers, claiming her lips, filling her with his tongue. He tasted so warm, so sweet, so strong. She wanted more of him. She couldn't get enough. And she didn't want to wait.

She broke off the kiss. She turned again to face the mirror, her back to him.

He watched her in the mirror, his eyes dark, intense, looking into her, waiting for what she'd do next.

She untied the sash at her waist. Fingers trembling, she pulled the sides of her robe apart and slipped it off her shoulders. She stood naked in front of him. Her breasts hung free, her nipples puckered and taut. Warmth curled between her legs.

He sucked in a long breath. She felt his gaze move over her as much as she saw it in the mirror. His eyes took in every detail, as if every inch of her skin was precious, every feature unique, the whole package more alluring than any woman he'd ever seen. "You are so beautiful."

She let his gaze and words and the feelings building inside engulf her. If she had this man looking at her just this way every day, she'd feel beautiful the rest of her life.

She'd feel wanted.

She pushed away a shiver of fear. She couldn't think of anything right now but him, the time they had together. She couldn't concentrate on anything but the reflection of his eyes.

Stepping forward, he pressed his body close once again. The ridge of his erection jutted against her bottom and lower back. The crisp fabric of his shirt rubbed against her.

Slipping his arms around her, he cupped her breasts in his hands, lifting, caressing. Her nipples poked between his fingers. Lowering his mouth, he kissed her neck, her shoulder. He slid one hand down her side and over her belly until he found the heat between her legs.

Her belly tightened, low and hot. A moan vibrated deep in her throat, a sound she didn't even recognize as her own. She rocked against him, the heat building. But she wanted more.

Reaching behind her, she gripped his shirt and pulled it from his pants. She wanted to feel his skin, his warmth. She needed all of him. She didn't want him to hold anything back.

He took his hands from her and stripped off his clothing. When he snuggled up behind her again, his skin smoothed warm against hers, his erection pressed against her, branding her with its heat. Nudging her legs apart, he moved closer, pushing between her thighs. But he didn't enter her. Instead he pressed tight against her. Taking a breast in each hand, he rubbed his tip across the most sensitive part of her.

Heat rippled through her, burgeoning with each stroke. She watched his hands lift her breasts, scissoring her nipples between his fingers. She felt the glow in his eyes, reveled in the hardness thrusting between her legs, rubbing, building. Pleasure shuddered through her and broke loose from her lips.

His strokes quickened, eliciting more shudders. Just when she thought she was done, he slipped inside her. He filled her, stretched her, yet she felt no pain. Only slick heat.

She watched him move into her. His eyes were

half closed, yet she could tell he was watching her, too. Watching her breasts bounce with each thrust. Watching the way she tilted her head back against him. Watching as the sounds of pleasure moaned deep in her throat.

He leaned forward, his breath tickling her ear. "I can't get enough of you, Sylvie. I could never get enough."

She soaked in the words, the sensations. She couldn't get enough of him, either. He was what she needed. What she'd always needed.

Slipping out of her, he scooped her into his arms and carried her out of the bathroom and laid her gently on the very edge of the bed. Nudging her legs apart, he settled between them and lowered his mouth to her.

She never guessed her body would still have the stamina to respond. He moved his mouth over her, devouring her until waves of shudders seized her again.

She cried out, louder this time. She could no longer control her response. She could no longer control her feelings.

Pressure bore down on her chest, making it hard to breathe. She was falling in love with him. It was too much, too fast, too dangerous, but she was falling in love with him anyway. Sometime tonight, she'd stepped over that cliff, and now she was plummeting. Now she would never be the same.

Chapter Fourteen

When Bryce awoke with sun peeking around the drapes and Sylvie curled at his side, he wasn't sure if he'd made a new start or a big mistake. All he knew was that he'd do it all over again in a heartbeat. When he'd told Sylvie she was the bravest and strongest woman he knew, he wasn't lying. Only now he'd have to add softest, sweetest, sexiest and most passionate to the list, as well.

He watched her eyes move under her closed lids, her hair spread over the pillow in wild waves. A smile played over her lips, the corners rising and falling with the flow of her dream. She looked so peaceful. More peaceful than she had since he'd met her. And he could only hope that he was a part of that.

He couldn't stand to see her as upset as she'd been last night. She hadn't wanted to admit it, but seeing Yamal dead had hit her hard, and he knew that ever-present fear for her sister was no small part of it. He probably shouldn't have come back to her room, shouldn't have asked her to open the bathroom door, shouldn't have kissed her, but he hadn't been able to stop himself. He hadn't wanted to stop himself. Now he only hoped that she didn't regret making love. That she knew how much he really cared about her.

He glanced across the room at the desk. The folder holding the articles about Dryden Kane that Diana had collected still perched under the lamp. Evidence of what he had been, what he had done. He hadn't shown them to Sylvie. He hadn't wanted her to know the truth. He hadn't wanted to see the look in her eyes. But after last night…

A tremor lodged in his chest. She might hate him. She might blame him for her sister's fate. Why wouldn't she? He sure as hell blamed himself. Though seeing condemnation in her eyes would rip him open, after last night he wanted to be honest. He wanted her to know him. And the only way for her to truly understand the man he had become was to know the man he once was.

He looked back to her sleeping face. So beautiful. So strong. So sweet. He bent over her and touched his lips to hers.

Her lids fluttered. Her eyes opened.

"Good morning."

At first she looked confused. Then she gave him a tentative smile. "What time is it?"

"Just after seven."

She moved to sit up, clutching the sheet to shield her breasts. "I need to call Perreth. I need to find out when the autopsy—"

He held up a hand. "Wait."

She sucked in a breath and looked at him, as if suddenly remembering what had passed between them. Or maybe she was just finally acknowledging it.

Something inside him hesitated. The connection between them was so tender, so new, anything could destroy it, much less what he was about to confess. But if it was to grow, he had to be honest. He lowered his lips to hers again, kissing her for what might be the last time. "We have to talk."

"About what?" Her eyes darted, searching his. "Last night?"

"Last night was more than I'd ever dreamed."

She let out a breath of relief.

"What I have to tell you happened long before last night."

She frowned, a crease digging between her eyebrows. "What?"

"I never really told you why I hate Dryden Kane so much. Why I need to find who's helping him. Why I need to set things right." He paused, searching for the words. How could he describe how single-minded he'd been? How ambitious? How caught up in the game of law? "Why don't I show you?"

Throwing back the sheets, he thrust himself out of bed. Naked, he crossed the floor to the desk and picked up the folder.

The shrill ring of the hotel phone cut through the room.

Sylvie sat up, pulling the sheet to her chest. She looked at the phone and then at him.

He could see the questions in her eyes, the fears. Was it Perreth with the lab results? With news of Diana? Was it the man in the ski mask?

Leaving the folder on the desk untouched, he crossed back to the bed. "Do you want me to answer?"

She shook her head. Taking a deep breath, she reached for the phone. She brought it to her ear, tilting it so Bryce could hear.

He sat on the edge of the bed and lowered his head next to hers.

Sylvie cleared her throat. "Hello?"

"Sylvie." The voice was weak, little more than a soft croak.

Tears pooled in the corners of Sylvie's eyes. "Reed. I'm so glad to hear your voice."

"Me, too. I had to call you myself. Can you come down here? We need to talk."

She nodded and looked to Bryce. "We'll be right there."

WHEN SYLVIE HAD HEARD Reed's voice over the phone, she was so relieved she could hardly speak. Now that Reed was awake, they'd find Diana for sure. Now that Reed was awake, Perreth would have to keep them in the loop. Now that Reed was awake, maybe she wouldn't feel so vulnerable. Maybe she could regain control.

But looking at Reed lying in the hospital bed in his private room—skin as white as the pillow his shaved head rested on, struggling for each molecule of oxygen from the tube threaded under his nose, as if he were alive and conscious by willpower alone—she wasn't so sure.

Sylvie stepped into the room. Bryce hung back, leaning against the jamb, as if to give her space to talk to Reed before she had to explain his presence. A consideration she appreciated.

Crossing to the bed, Sylvie realized they weren't alone. Giving the woman standing in the corner of the room a passing glance and nod, Sylvie stopped at Reed's bedside and focused on him. "How are you feeling?"

The corner of his lips twitched in a smile. "Great."

At least he hadn't lost his sense of humor. She took his hand in hers, carefully skirting the IV needle, and gave him a teasing smile that she didn't feel. "I thought you were dead."

"If you hadn't found me so quickly, I might be."

So quickly? She hadn't been quick. She'd been too late. "I wish I would have found you a lot quicker than I did."

"Why? So the bastard could have kidnapped you, too?"

"So you know Diana is gone."

He glanced at the woman in the corner. "Yes."

Sylvie followed his gaze.

With long, lush brunette hair and a face that could grace magazine covers, the woman should be beautiful. But there was something hard about her—a sharp glint in her eyes, a brittle tension to her lips— something hungry that undermined her striking looks and made Sylvie a little uncomfortable.

"Sylvie, this is Nikki Valducci," Reed said. "She started working with me last week."

The woman stepped across the room and offered Sylvie her hand. "I just got my promotion to detective, and Reed was supposed to be teaching me the ropes. Instead, I'm here delivering him flowers." She nodded at a basket of carnations and baby's breath.

"And news," added Reed.

"Yes."

Sylvie reassessed Reed's new partner. She liked that hard hunger in a cop. Especially a cop who was working with Reed, a cop who would help her find Diana. "Glad to meet you." Sylvie took her hand.

Nikki shook hands with gusto, the entire time standing in the characteristic stance of a cop, the right leg slightly back to protect her gun side.

Sylvie nodded toward the door. "Reed and Nikki, this is Bryce."

Bryce shared a nod with the detectives.

"He's been helping me." It seemed like such a lame explanation, one that didn't even begin to describe her relationship with Bryce. But then, she wasn't sure of her relationship with Bryce, so how could she describe it to others?

She steered her mind away from the questions clouding her mind, questions about last night, about what it was that Bryce had felt he had to tell her this morning.

"Stan Perreth says you've been searching for Diana."

She focused on Reed, taking his hand in hers once again. "We haven't found her." Had Detective Perreth told Reed about the body the police had found? The body they thought was Diana's?

She watched Reed's eyes, the paleness of his face. If she was in his place, no matter how weak she was, she'd want to know. She was pretty sure he would, too. "Did Perreth tell you about the burned body?"

"Nikki did. That's part of what I need to talk to you about."

A cold sweat slicked Sylvie's back and trickled

between her shoulder blades. The DNA test? Did he know the results?

Bryce crossed the waxed tile and stopped beside her.

She didn't look up at him. She couldn't. She knew why he'd moved beside her. To take care of her if the news was bad. To be there for her if...

She shook her head and focused on Reed's dark eyes. "The lab was doing a DNA test and..." She couldn't finish. All she could do was stand there and hope her silence conveyed the rest.

"Didn't Perreth tell you?" Reed's voice rose in anger, despite his condition.

Sylvie's pulse rang in her ears. "Did he get the results?"

"It's not a match. Not even close." He gave her hand a squeeze. "I'm so sorry he didn't tell you. The results came this morning. They didn't even have to do a DNA test. The blood type didn't match yours. The body's not Diana's. Diana might still be alive."

Sylvie's knees sagged like rubber.

Bryce placed a hand on her elbow, steadying her.

She gave him a grateful glance. She could handle this. If Diana was still alive, she could handle anything. "Then we have to find her."

Nikki gave Reed a pointed look. "If she didn't know about the test, she doesn't know the rest, either."

"The rest?" Her mind crested relief and plummeted back into worry, as if she was riding a roller coaster.

"I'll tell her," Nikki said.

Reed exhaled heavily and leaned his head back on his pillow. If possible, he looked worse than he had when they'd arrived.

Nikki turned her razor-sharp eyes on Sylvie. "The past few months, we—or rather, Reed, along with some county detectives—have been investigating two murders in the area. Both murders had certain characteristics in common."

"Like what?" Sylvie gripped Reed's hand, balling her other hand into a fist by her side. All she had to do was to look at the despair in Reed's eyes to know whatever Nikki was getting to was vitally important.

"Both of the victims were women, for one thing. Both were killed with a serrated knife. And there were other similarities, too, things that weren't released to the press."

"Can you get to the point?"

Nikki nodded to acknowledge Bryce's question, yet kept her focus on Sylvie. "The body Perreth thought was your sister's matched most of these characteristics."

Sylvie thought of the reasons Perreth had given for not letting her see the body. "All the women were burned and had their teeth pulled?"

"No. That's where this body differed. That's why

we didn't identify the last murder as part of the pattern, at least not right away."

Bryce frowned. "And what makes you think it's part of the pattern now?"

"Virtually everything else about the murder matches. And the other elements of this killer's signature are very distinctive."

"Signature?" Sylvie had skimmed enough articles about Dryden Kane to know what that word signified. "Are you talking about a serial killer here?"

Nikki exchanged glances with Reed. "Yes."

A serial killer. Sylvie flinched at the thought of the photos of Dryden Kane's victims. The young blond women. The woman who looked like Diana, like her. The familiar hum grew louder in her ears. "Why are you telling us this?"

"The killer's signature is identical to a killer who struck Wisconsin a number of years ago."

His name stuck in Sylvie's throat.

"Dryden Kane," Bryce supplied.

Nikki nodded.

"But he's in prison." Sylvie's voice barely rose above a whisper. The image of Diana running through the forest lodged in her mind. Diana being hunted like an animal, the way Dryden Kane had done with most of his victims. Frustration and fear twisted her stomach and clogged her throat. "Isn't he in prison?"

"Yes. He's still at Banesbridge. It isn't Kane

himself. But whoever this is seems to be copying his signature nearly exactly. A copycat killer."

Sylvie's mind jumped ahead—to why Nikki was telling her this, to what it had to do with her. With Diana. "They're all blond, aren't they? The three women?"

"Yes."

"And they look like Kane's original victims? The women he killed before his escape?"

"Yes."

She thought of the scenario she and Bryce had discussed. "Do you suspect Kane is controlling this copycat? Controlling him from his prison cell?"

"We don't really know. But we think it's possible. The copycat killer is reproducing details about Kane's murders that only someone privy to the case files would know."

"Like a detective." Sylvie glanced at Bryce.

"Or someone who devoted his life to studying Kane," Bryce countered.

Suddenly, Sylvie knew why Nikki was telling her about these murders. "Diana. You're afraid that Diana..." She couldn't finish, but she didn't have to. Reed's nod told her all she needed to know.

"Oh, my God." She sucked in a breath, fighting for control.

Bryce grabbed her arm as if he was afraid she'd go down.

Regaining her balance, she swung her focus to Reed. "Do you know about the research project? The interviews Diana was doing with Dryden Kane?"

"Nikki told me this morning."

Nikki told him. Not Diana. Diana had been keeping her fascination with Kane a secret from Reed, too. "The two professors she was working with? We found out one of them was pursuing Diana. She complained to his supervising professor. He's been studying Kane for years. He knows everything there is to know about him."

"Sami Yamal committed suicide," Bryce added. "We found his body yesterday. If he's the copycat killer, he's dead."

Sylvie sucked in a breath. It wasn't that simple. It wasn't that simple at all. "If Sami *was* the copycat killer, we might never find Diana. Even if she's still alive…"

She couldn't let herself panic. She had to keep what little control she had. She had to find out exactly what Reed and Nikki knew and what they didn't. "You think Kane is behind this, right?"

"Yes," Nikki answered. "We're still exploring other possibilities. But judging from the evidence, Kane seems to be pulling the strings."

Bryce slipped an arm around her. His body pressed against her side, solid, close. But she couldn't take comfort in his presence this time. She couldn't take comfort in anything.

She'd been so naive through all this. Purposefully so. She'd stubbornly clung to the hope that she'd be able to find Diana. That she'd be able to get her sister back alive. She'd really believed that Bryce could help her get the answers she needed. She'd believed that once Reed awakened they could work together to save her sister, to get her back. But the truth was, an entire law firm of Bryces and a whole department of Reeds and Nikkis couldn't find Diana. If what they said was true, only she had a shot at doing that.

She pulled away from Bryce's side. Forcing steel into her spine, she focused on Nikki Valducci. "I want you to set up a meeting for me."

"A meeting?"

"I'm going to talk to Dryden Kane."

Chapter Fifteen

Sylvie's words crashed down on Bryce's skull with the force of a sledgehammer. She couldn't be suggesting what she was suggesting. She couldn't. "You're not meeting with him."

Sylvie balled her hands into fists by her sides, as if readying for a knock-down-drag-out. "It's not your choice to make."

"It might not be mine to make, but that doesn't mean it's one *you* should make. He's dangerous. You can't walk into that prison and have a chat with a monster like that. It's like waving a red flag in front of a rabid bull."

"Even if the copycat isn't Sami Yamal, he already knows I'm Diana's sister. He's already tried to kidnap me. I'm already a target. Talking to Kane isn't going to make any difference."

"You think Kane is going to tell you where Diana

is? You think he's going to call off his copycat if you ask nicely?"

"I might learn something from him. Something that could help."

"Learn something?" Bryce couldn't believe his ears. He looked to Reed and his partner. "You can't let her do this."

"Why not? Why are you acting like I'm not in danger already? Why are you acting like this will change anything? You were there. If you hadn't gotten me out of that van, I'd be with the copycat right now. I have nothing to lose."

"You have your life to lose."

"You're not listening to me."

"You're right. I'm not listening. And if listening means thinking what you're proposing is a good idea, I'll sure as hell *never* listen." He glared at Reed. "You have to tell her to forget it."

"He's right, Sylvie. Kane is a manipulator. A sadist. He won't give you any answers if he can help it. He'd only try to cause you pain."

"And having some copycat killer kidnap my sister and hunt her down like an animal while I do nothing isn't causing me pain?"

Reed looked at Sylvie with troubled eyes. "I understand you're desperate, Sylvie. God, I'm desperate, too. But putting yourself in the same situation as Diana isn't going to help her."

"I won't be in the same situation. I'll be ready for him. I'll have protection." She looked to Nikki. "Right?"

Nikki glanced at Reed. Apparently she knew enough not to answer.

Sylvie circled Reed's bed and approached his partner. "You can see where I'm going with this idea, can't you? From a purely objective point of view? I mean, law enforcement uses family members help with cases like this, doesn't it? At least sometimes?"

"She's got a point," Nikki said.

Bryce sprang toward her. Had she lost her mind, too? "A point? She's talking about going toe-to-toe with a serial killer and you say she's got a point?"

She ignored him, keeping her eyes on her partner. "What's wrong with using a little proactive approach? I mean, really. If she was anyone else, we'd probably take her up on the offer. We'd let her talk to him and make sure she was protected. She needs to be put under police protection anyway."

Sylvie nodded as if buoyed by Nikki's support. "If we don't do something, more women might die. Diana might die."

Thunder rose in Bryce's ears. "Have you both gone crazy? This man is dangerous." Bryce crossed the floor in two strides.

Sylvie glanced up at him, her chin jutting slightly, her eyes determined.

He grasped her arms, forcing her to look into his eyes. He had to make her see what she was getting into. He had to keep her from going through with this insane plan. "I understand what you're going through, Sylvie, but you can't talk to Kane."

"No, you don't understand. How could you?"

If only he'd had more time this morning before Reed called. Then she would understand. "Because if there were a chance my brother was still alive, I'd risk everything to save him."

"But I won't be risking everything. You heard Nikki. The police will protect me. Kane won't be able to hurt me."

His throat felt thick, hot. He couldn't swallow. He couldn't speak. He was not going to lose Sylvie to that monster. He was not going to let Kane take her the way he'd taken Ty. "I need to talk to you."

"We *are* talking."

"Alone. Now."

"I'm not going to change my mind."

"Please. Just hear me out. Give me that much."

She glanced at Reed and Nikki. Finally she nodded.

Still holding one of her arms, Bryce led her out of the room. Privacy. They needed someplace private. He didn't want the whole hospital to hear what he was about to say.

Weaving through a maze of hallways, he negotiated his way to the rooftop deck. Sun sparkled off the two main lakes and bathed the narrow isthmus of buildings stretching between. Not far away, the capitol dome caught the sun. The golden statue on its pinnacle stabbed into a blue sky.

If only they had ventured up here to enjoy the day. If only there was no cold current of wind undercutting the sunny view. Wind that chilled him to the bone.

Leaning against the rail, Sylvie wrapped her arms around herself. She squinted up at him. "Okay. Talk."

He shrugged out of his coat and attempted to drape it over her shoulders.

She held up a hand. "I don't need your coat. I need to hear what you wanted to say. What you couldn't say inside."

"I wanted to tell you this morning, when you woke up." He draped his coat over the rail. His chest ached with each breath. His throat pinched, the words he had to say strangling him. But he had to get them out. He had no pictures, no articles to explain it for him this time. "Yesterday you asked about Kane's lawyer."

Her eyebrows pulled together. "What about him?"

"I *am* Kane's lawyer. Or at least, I was until about six weeks ago."

She didn't move, didn't gasp, nothing. She just stared at him with steady eyes, waiting for him to go on, waiting for him to explain.

"When the lawsuits against the Supermax prison started a few years ago, I decided to get in on it. I decided it would give the law firm some press, bring in more clients."

"But Kane? Why Kane?"

"Because he would bring the biggest headlines." The picture he was painting for her made him feel sick, but he couldn't stop. It was the truth. He had been that man, chasing headlines, chasing notoriety, playing with the law like it was a game. He had been that man so wrapped up in his own greed and ambition that he couldn't see anything else.

"And this is what you wanted to tell me?"

"No. I mean, yes, but it's not everything."

She hugged herself tighter. "What else?"

He pulled a breath into aching lungs. He had to continue. "I won the suit against the Supermax. I got Kane a transfer to another facility. But he didn't merely want less restrictive conditions, less solitary. That wasn't enough for Kane."

"What did he want?"

Bryce looked out at the skyline, at the blue curves of the lakes. He'd gotten Kane nearly everything he'd asked for, everything he didn't deserve. "He wasn't happy with Banesbridge. It's an old prison, just starting to be renovated. But it's very secure. There's never been an escape."

"He wanted something less secure, didn't he?"

Bryce nodded. "He escaped from Grantsville. He was looking for a place he could escape from again." He remembered the grin on Kane's thin lips when he'd made his demand clear. And the sense of anger under the surface when Bryce hadn't come through. He could remember every moment with Kane, as vivid in his mind as if he'd seen the monster this morning.

"So what happened?"

"When I refused to get him another transfer, he threatened me."

Sylvie's eyes flared with alarm. "What did you do?"

"Nothing." And he'd never forgive himself for it. "I underestimated him. He was in prison. He couldn't get out. He couldn't hurt me from behind bars."

Sylvie's throat moved under tender skin, as if she was struggling to swallow all he'd told her, trying to prepare for what came next.

Bryce had never been able to prepare. He'd never seen it coming. "He killed my brother. He killed Ty. And the whole thing was my damn fault."

"Kane killed your brother?"

"He had him killed. I'm guessing by the same guy who's killing these women."

"The case you talked about, the reason you hate Kane, it was all about your brother's murder."

"Yes." She hadn't asked a question, but he needed to answer anyway. He needed to make sure everything was clear.

He waited for that look he dreaded. One of disgust. Horror. Condemnation. The one he'd seen in the mirror every morning for the past six weeks.

It never came. Instead she stepped close and put her arms around him. "I'm sorry, Bryce. I'm so sorry."

Pain pressed behind his eyes and knifed through his sinuses. He hadn't expected sympathy from Sylvie. He'd expected a lot of things, but not this. As much as he thought of her, as much as he cared about her, he'd underestimated her. "I love you, Sylvie. God, I love you."

She peered up at him, moisture glistening in her eyes.

He couldn't lose her. Now that he'd found her, he couldn't let her go. "Don't do this. Please. Promise you'll stay away from him."

Tears spiked her lashes and trickled down her cheeks. "I know how awful this must be for you, Bryce. I understand now."

His throat closed. He knew where she was leading before she said the words. He knew her decision would scar her forever. And if he lost her because of it, it would destroy him.

"But I need you to understand me, too."

SYLVIE SHIFTED on the plain wooden chair. Crossing and uncrossing her legs, she finally settled on crossing her ankles, knees pressed tightly together.

She'd never been inside the walls of a prison before. And even though she was in main building, far from the cell blocks, she already she knew she never wanted to come to a place like this again. She didn't mind the Spartan room, furnished with only a scarred table and four chairs, one bolted to the floor. She didn't mind the antiseptic smell. She didn't even mind the dour-faced guards. What she hated was the sound of doors locking behind them as they passed through the sally ports. And that no matter how deeply she inhaled, she couldn't seem to breathe.

She glanced at the camera in the corner of the room. Bryce was watching through that camera, worrying with Nikki Valducci and several detectives Sylvie didn't know. He had insisted on coming with her, a demand that made her eyes burn. She knew this was hell for him, seeing the man responsible for killing his brother, the man he hated, watching her face that man. The fact that he'd come with her, stuck by her even through this, made her heart squeeze. She only hoped it wasn't all in vain, that she could coax some answers from Dryden Kane, answers that would lead to finding Diana.

The door opened. Two uniformed guards stepped into the room, and between them, hands and feet shackled, shuffled Dryden Kane.

He looked much like his photograph, only older. Brown hair now silver, he appeared as if he should be wearing a nice suit or a relaxed weekend baseball shirt, not the baggy prison jumpsuit. Although he was clearly in his fifties, the boyish quality she'd noticed in his photograph was still there. The slightly weak slant to his chin, the disarming arch to his eyebrows—all of it conspired to make him appear more like the quintessential next-door neighbor than an infamous killer. He raised his eyes to hers.

His eyes were like his picture, too. Ice blue. And void of emotion.

She suppressed a shiver.

The corners of thin lips lifted in a smile. "Sylvie. You're as beautiful as your sister."

Diana. That was the reason she was here. To find her sister. To enlist Kane's help. "I want to talk to you about Diana."

He lowered himself into the chair.

Shackles rattling, the guards handcuffed his hands to the steel rails. One of the guards gave her a pointed look. "Are you sure you don't want one of us to stay in here with you?"

Of course she did. Better yet, she wanted Bryce and the detectives in here, as well, not merely watching from the next room. "I'll be fine."

"Of course you will be," Kane said, voice low and melodic. "I'm no animal, despite what they imply with their handcuffs and chains. I'm well-read, civilized. I know how to treat a lady."

Sylvie resisted the urge to look at the camera, to reassure herself that Bryce was there, just steps away. That she wasn't alone. Only she could do this now. And no one could help her. She folded her hands in her lap, picking at the edges of her fingernails. "I'm not sure how to ask this."

"I've found the direct approach is best."

Right. And she'd be willing to bet Kane was as direct as a crazy straw. "I'm glad you feel that way."

He smiled, thin lips pulling back to reveal straight white teeth. She caught a whiff of mint mouthwash, as if he'd gargled just for her.

"My sister has disappeared."

His smile faded. "When?"

"Saturday afternoon. Someone kidnapped her from her wedding. Do you know where she is?"

His eyebrows dipped low. A muscle twitched in his clean-shaven cheek. "Why would you think I know anything? If you haven't noticed, I don't get out much."

"That wasn't a direct answer."

"Forgive me. I'm a bit shaken by the news."

He looked about as shaken as a professional poker player. "I'm worried about Diana. I've come here for your help."

"My help." A smile curved the corners of his lips, as if he liked the idea.

"Yes."

"That is as it should be, isn't it?"

As it should be? Clearly he liked the position of power that her coming to him for help gave him. Power over her. But although the thought of giving this man any kind of power over her turned her stomach, she had to submit. She had to do whatever it took to find Diana. "Will you help me find my sister?"

He leaned back in his chair. "I'm sorry I have to let you down, Sylvie. But I don't know where your sister is."

"Please. I know you're a powerful man. I know you're in touch with someone outside of prison."

"You think I asked someone to take Diana?"

"Did you?"

Closing his eyes, he shook his head. "I'm disappointed you would think that. I expected more from you."

She wouldn't let him manipulate her. She wouldn't let him throw her off track. "Please answer my question."

"I didn't have anything to do with your sister's disappearance. I have no reason to want to hurt her."

Too bad she didn't believe him. "Three women have been murdered recently."

He lifted an eyebrow in surprise.

The gesture felt forced. "They were killed in the same way you killed your victims. The same exact way."

"And what way is that?"

Did he want her to describe the murders? To voice the horrible things he'd done? The thought made her sick. "I don't think you need me to tell you what you already know."

"No. But I do need you to tell me why you think Diana is among these women. That's why you're here, right? You think Diana is one of them? Or you're afraid she will be?"

"Is she?"

"I don't know anything about these women you speak of, but I can assure you that I have no reason to hurt your sister."

Except that Diana looked like the wife he murdered.

"You don't look convinced."

"I've seen pictures of the women you killed. Pictures of your wife. Diana looks just like her."

"Yes, Adrianna." A gleam lit his eyes that made Sylvie want to bolt for the door. "Diana does look like her. Of course, you do, too."

She swallowed and forced herself to meet those cold eyes. "These other three women are blond, too."

"Oh?" Another raise of the eyebrows in feigned surprise.

Maybe Bryce was right. Maybe she'd been stupid to think she'd get any answers from Dryden Kane. Maybe the smart thing would be for her to walk out that door and forget she'd ever laid eyes on the serial killer. But she couldn't do that. She had to give it one last try. "Help me find Diana. Please, Mr. Kane."

He narrowed his eyes. "Hmm. That's not right."

"Not right? What isn't right?"

"You calling me Mr. Kane. I don't like it."

She'd call him babycakes if that was what it took to win his cooperation. "Would you like me to call you Dryden?"

He shook his head. "That's not right, either."

Frustration knotted in her gut, replacing the edgy feeling of nausea. She knew Kane was a manipulator, that he would play with her emotions every chance he got. She wished she could be cool, detached, beat him at his own game, but she couldn't. She needed him. "Please, where is Diana?"

"I told you, I don't know where she is. I wish I did. Believe me, I'm as worried about her as you are."

She ground her teeth together. She was getting mighty tired of his false charm. She felt like spitting in his face. "I can tell you're eaten up with worry."

"Sylvie, Sylvie, there's no reason for sarcasm." He shook his head as if he was disappointed. "I can tell you what I know about your sister. Maybe that will help you see that I mean what I say."

She knew better than to expect him to tell her anything of value. He was just playing her again. But she found herself leaning forward in her chair nonetheless. "What do you know?"

"I know she's beautiful, like you. She's smart, like you. But that isn't surprising, is it? Not with identical twins." He leaned back in his chair and looked past her at the wall, as if lost in private thoughts.

Sylvie clasped her hands together to keep them from shaking. She dug at the edges of her fingernails, picking at her cuticles. What was he thinking about? Times during Diana's interviews with him when he manipulated her like he was trying to manipulate Sylvie? Or was he fantasizing about the hell Diana was going through now?

"Diana had this puppet she liked to play with. A Mexican clown. She loved that thing. She never let it out of her sight. It was her favorite, along with the music box. You both loved the music box."

Sylvie narrowed her eyes on Kane. What was he talking about? Had he lost his mind? Slipped into some kind of delusional fantasy world? The articles she'd read about Kane stated that he wasn't insane, but if this rambling wasn't insanity, what was it? "Excuse me?"

"You, of course, were too sick for puppets." He shifted his stare back to her. "I was worried about you. I'm glad to see you so strong. You turned out as beautiful and strong as your sister."

Her mind stuttered. She struggled to grasp what he was saying. "I don't understand."

"Of course you don't. You were too young. Young

but sweet. You used to look up to me like I was a god. You made me feel like a god. That's when I realized things were all wrong. That I had to change my life. I had to take control."

Her throat constricted, making it hard to swallow, hard to speak. "I'm sorry, Mr. Kane. I don't know what you're talking about."

"Didn't I tell you I don't want you calling me Mr. Kane?"

"I'm sorry."

He shifted in his chair, chains rattling. His eyes glinted like glittering ice. "Do you know what I want you to call me, Sylvie? Have you figured it out yet?"

"What?" Her voice was only a whisper, but suddenly she wished she could take the word back. She wished she could jump from her chair and race out of the room. She wished she'd never set foot in this prison, never heard of Dryden Kane.

But as much as she wanted to change the past, she couldn't. Nor could she alter what would happen next. She waited for him to tell her the name, feeling as powerless to stop him as a three-year-old.

His thin lips spread into a slow smile. "Daddy. I want you to call me Daddy."

Chapter Sixteen

Bryce threw the door open and pushed into the prison's interview room. He had to get Sylvie out of here. Away from this monster. Kane had gone too far. Much too far. "This meeting is over."

Nikki Valducci and a balding county detective named Mylinski stepped into the room behind him along with two guards.

Sylvie didn't look up. She didn't move. She just stared at her hands, as if she didn't hear him, as if she didn't know any of them were there. She dug compulsively at the edges of her fingernails, as if as long as she could control the offending cuticles, she could control the situation.

"Hello, counselor."

Bryce clenched his jaw until it ached. He kept his eyes on Sylvie. He didn't dare look in Kane's direction. One look at that smirk and Bryce wasn't sure he could prevent himself from choking the life out of him.

"All right, Kane," one of the guards said in a bored voice. "Your fun is done for the day. Time to go back to your cell."

"Sylvie?" Bryce said in a gentle voice.

Sylvie didn't look up.

He knelt beside her and grasped her hands, stopping the frantic movement of her fingers. "Sylvie?"

She moved her gaze to his face, but he couldn't sense any kind of a connection looking into her eyes. She seemed to be staring through him at another world. A world very far away.

She must be in shock. Why the hell wouldn't she be? He sure was. He didn't know what to think, what to feel, what to believe. Astonishment, denial, and anger tangled inside him like a writhing snake. But he couldn't sort it out now. He had to focus, to keep himself together until after he got Sylvie far away from Dryden Kane.

"Let's get out of here, Sylvie. Come on." Gently he pulled her up out of her chair.

"Think twice before trusting a lawyer, Sylvie. Especially this one." Kane's voice prodded him like a blunt stick poking at a wounded animal. "He's the type that will use you to further his own agenda. A truly manipulative and selfish breed."

Bryce ground his teeth until his jaw hurt. "If I were you, Kane, I'd shut the hell up. You're an awfully stationary target."

"What kind of a daddy would I be if I didn't offer my little girl some fatherly advice?"

Rage rang in Bryce's ears, pushing him closer to the edge. Kane couldn't be Sylvie's father. He wouldn't believe it. And if that bastard didn't shut up he'd put his hands on either side of his head and snap his neck like a twig. Avenge Ty's death. Make him pay for all he'd done. The justice of it tasted so sweet on his tongue, it was all he could do to force his feet to step toward the door. "Come on, Sylvie. Don't listen to him. He's just trying to hurt you."

"I would never hurt Sylvie. She's my daughter, Walker. My little girl."

No. No. No.

Sylvie stopped, she turned to face Kane. "My mother. She was your wife?"

"Adrianna." He shook his head. "We could have been the perfect little family. But unlike you and your sister, she didn't understand me. She never did."

Bryce angled his body between Kane and Sylvie. He pulled her toward the door.

She hesitated.

"Come on, Sylvie."

"Maybe she doesn't want to go with you, Walker. Maybe she wants to stay and talk. She hasn't seen her daddy in twenty years."

"Go to hell, Kane."

"Eventually. And when I get there, I'll be sure to say hello to Ty for you."

Bryce let go of Sylvie's hand. Dodging around the cops, he launched himself at Kane and slammed a fist into the bastard's nose.

Cartilage gave under his knuckles. Kane's head snapped back. A spray of blood misted the air, hot and sticky.

Hands clawed at Bryce, grabbing him, pinning his arms behind his back. Nikki Valducci and the balding cop dragged him away from Kane.

"I wish I could let you at him," the balding detective said, dipping his lips close to Bryce's ear. "You'd be doing the world a favor."

Once he'd dragged Bryce clear of the room, the detective released his arms. "Go on, take her out of here." He stepped back into the interview room, closing the door behind him.

Sylvie stared up at Bryce, questions brimming in her eyes.

Bryce clenched his hands into fists. His head throbbed. His mouth tasted of blood. How could Dryden Kane be Sylvie's father? How did any of this make sense?

She needed his help. He could see it in her eyes. In their desperate shine behind squinting lashes. She needed his help to sort through the shock, to understand what had just happened, to figure out what it meant.

Pressure built in his head. He groped inside himself. For something to give her, a word, a touch. But all that was there was the empty echo of Ty's laugh. The scent of blood. And the smug look in Dryden Kane's eyes.

He had to get out of here. Away from Kane. Away from the bitter burn in his heart. And, God forgive him, even away from Sylvie.

Dryden Kane's daughter.

"I'm sorry, Sylvie." He strode for the sally port and the hall beyond.

SYLVIE LEANED BACK in the passenger seat of the police cruiser and struggled to catch her breath. She'd thought that once she emerged from behind the prison walls, behind the tall fences topped with curls of razor wire, she would be able to breathe. She couldn't have been more wrong.

They'd been driving for more than a hour, the officer assigned to take her back to her hotel relating one story after another. Normal stories of dogs giving birth and children mispronouncing words, stories to cling to like a concrete mooring. But still her chest ached. Still her lungs refused to fill with air. And no matter how many short gasps she took, she couldn't get the oxygen she needed.

She might have left Kane back at the prison, but she could never escape him. She didn't know why, but she knew he was telling the truth, if only about being her father. He was part of her past. Part of her DNA. Every time she looked in the mirror, she'd see his eyes. Every time she saw a father laughing with his daughter, she'd hear his voice.

Daddy. I want you to call me Daddy.

She shuddered. She hadn't picked her cuticles bloody since she was five years old, when her foster mother had wrapped each finger with a bandage to force Sylvie to break the habit. But they were raw now. Bloody. Drops stained her skin and soaked into her jeans.

When Dryden Kane had told her he was her father, she thought she'd hit bottom. She was wrong about that, too. She hadn't known what bottom was until she'd seen the look in Bryce's eyes.

She wrapped her arms around herself, gripping her sweater's chunky knit with both hands. Her fingertips stung like a bright light. Pain she welcomed. Pain she could hold on to. Pain that blotted the images of Bryce and Kane and the ugly secret Diana had kept from her mind.

The officer wound the car through Madison streets, negotiating one after another until the hotel peeked over neighboring buildings.

She didn't want to go back there. Didn't want to step into that room. The room where she'd given herself to Bryce. The room where she'd thought she was in love.

She wished she could cry, let the tears wash away

the memories, the betrayals, the feelings she'd conjured out of loneliness and longing, but her eyes remained dry. She didn't have enough tears left. She would never have enough tears.

The officer pulled the car into the mouth of the hotel's underground garage. After stopping for the attendant, he continued into the cavernous structure. Fluorescent light cast a green pall over the few vehicles inside. Pulling the car into a parking spot near the elevator, the officer switched off the engine and scanned the surrounding vehicles. "Let's get you up to that room."

It sounded like a prison sentence. Like torture. But Sylvie had no choice. She couldn't run. She couldn't hide. Not from who she was. Not from the secrets Diana kept. Not from what she'd wanted to believe she'd found with Bryce, what the look in his eyes told her she'd never found at all.

She and the officer opened their doors and climbed from the car. Something moved in front of them, shifting in the shadows of the garage. Sylvie jolted and turned. Trying to spot it. Trying to see what it was.

A red jacket. A ski mask.

Before she could react, a shot split the air.

The officer slumped against the car. Clawing at his holster with frantic fingers, he slipped down the driver's door and landed on the floor.

Sylvie screamed. She tried to run. But he was on top of her. An arm crashed down on her shoulder. Her legs buckled, sending her sprawling on the concrete.

A strong arm clamped her wrist and pulled her arm behind her back. Pain knifed through her shoulder. The prick of a needle sank into her flesh.

She twisted and kicked. Fighting for her life. Trying to get away before the fog closed around her like thick cotton batting. Before the world faded away.

Chapter Seventeen

Bryce had done a lot of stupid things in his life, but walking out on Sylvie at the prison topped the list. Hours of driving along curving highways and over rolling hills might not have done a damn thing to clear his mind or to sort through the emotions raging inside him, but it had given him the chance to cool off, to shake the shock out of his system and recognize what a dumb ass he'd been.

Dryden Kane might have destroyed the rest of Bryce's life, but even Kane couldn't destroy the love Bryce had found with Sylvie. Of course, he hadn't needed to. By walking out on her just when she needed him most, Bryce had accomplished that all on his own.

He turned down a one-way street and wound his way toward the hotel. He doubted she'd want to see him. All he knew was that he *had* to see her. Talk to her. Hold her. Maybe then he could sort through the jumble in his mind. Maybe then he'd know how to make things right.

He swung the BMW around the last turn. The hotel loomed in front of him, its slick stone exterior and glass entrance awash in the flashing red and blue lights of half a dozen police cars.

Sylvie.

He swung the BMW to the curb in front of a fire hydrant and climbed out. He launched into a run, racing for the hotel. He made it as far as the sidewalk in front of the parking garage entrance before a young uniformed cop stopped him. "Whoa, whoa, whoa! This is a crime scene. No one's allowed beyond this point."

"A crime scene?" That was why the police were here. That was why lights throbbed from police cruisers and yellow tape cordoned off the garage. Somehow he knew all this, yet the words *crime scene* still sent a shock wave through him. They still made him feel weak in the knees.

Visions of Sylvie bloodied and dead flashed in his mind. He shut the images out. He wouldn't think that way. He couldn't. He focused on the officer barring his way. "I need to talk to someone in charge."

"Did you see something?"

"No."

"Then I'm sorry, sir. The detectives are very busy. Leave your contact information with me, and I'll make sure they get it."

"I have information that might help."

The officer looked at him sideways, as if he sensed a lie. "If you leave your phone number—"

"Is Nikki Valducci here? Stan Perreth?"

"Like I said, the detectives are busy."

"You have to let me through. I have to talk to them."

The cop shook his head.

Bryce knew the officer was only doing his job securing the crime scene, but that didn't keep him from wanting to punch the guy right in his fresh, rule-reciting mouth. "Listen, I'm an attorney. The woman under police protection, she's my client." *His client.* Funny, but Sylvie was never his client, not officially. But she was so much more.

"I still can't let you through, sir. Only the detectives and technicians working the case can go beyond this point."

Bryce looked past the young cop, searching the garage's yawning mouth for Nikki or Perreth. But though he saw movement inside, he couldn't find anyone he recognized. He focused on the young cop. "What's going on? What happened?"

The cop shifted his feet.

Great. The kid probably aced Keeping Your Mouth Shut 101 at the police academy. "My client wasn't hurt, was she?"

"No." He dragged out the word.

So Sylvie wasn't hurt, but there was more. More

the officer didn't want to share. "Is she missing? Was she kidnapped?"

He pressed his lips together, as if trying to prevent himself from blurting out an answer.

Oh, God, she was. He could tell by the officer's body language. "How? How did he get her?" And more importantly, *Where had he taken her?*

"I'm sorry. If you want to leave your contact information, the detectives can—"

"Yeah, yeah, here." Reaching into his pocket, he pulled out a business card and shoved it at the cop. "Tell Nikki Valducci to call me. Tell her it's urgent."

The cop nodded.

Bryce marched back to his car, his mind racing. Calling Perreth would be a waste of time. Every time he'd dialed the number, he'd had to make do with the detective's voice mail. Not that Perreth would be a font of information. No doubt he was the young cop's mentor when it came to tight lips.

He opened his car door and slid behind the wheel. Sylvie was gone. He couldn't let himself panic. He couldn't let himself contemplate the worst. He had to think. He had to find her. He sure as hell wasn't going to lose Sylvie the way he lost Ty.

How could Kane do this? Sylvie had left him less than two hours ago. How had he ordered his lackey to strike this quickly?

Bryce leaned back in the seat. The timing wasn't

the only thing that was strange. The whole situation didn't feel right.

Sylvie and Diana weren't merely blondes who looked like Kane's wife. They were his daughters, his blood. Why would Kane strike out at them for no reason? Why would he order some lackey to kidnap and kill them as if they meant nothing?

Was he that depraved? That arbitrary?

Never in a million years would Bryce believe Kane *loved* Sylvie and Diana, but even Kane did things for reasons. Twisted, sick reasons, but reasons nonetheless. And the way Kane had acted with Sylvie in the prison didn't suggest resentment, hatred, aggression. He'd wanted to charm her. He'd wanted to manipulate her. And he'd certainly wanted her to know he was her father. But beyond the emotional trauma of learning her father was a serial killer, Kane hadn't seemed to want to hurt her.

So how did it make sense for him to order her kidnapping? Her death?

It didn't.

Bryce started the car. The professor. He needed to talk to Professor Bertram. Maybe he could shed some light. He'd studied the serial killer for years. He was the expert. He knew all about Kane.

He knew all about Kane.

The thought hit Bryce with the force of a kick to the gut.

If the professor was as knowledgeable as he claimed, wouldn't he know that Kane had three-year-old twin daughters at the time that he killed his wife? And wasn't it possible he'd found out who those now-adult daughters were?

He thought of the letter addressed to Diana, the letter they'd thought was from Kane. But what if it wasn't from Kane at all? What if it was from Bertram? What if he'd wanted Diana Gale to pay for the crimes of her father?

Bryce's heart beat high in his chest. The professor's sunken eyes and rumpled appearance of the day before flashed through his mind. He'd seemed upset, desperate. Could he have been losing it? Could years of trying to learn the reason behind his daughter's death only to be toyed with by a cruel manipulator have taken their toll?

God knows in just minutes Kane had gotten to Bryce. He'd pushed him so far, he'd forgotten everything but his hatred, his need for revenge. He'd turned his back on his own happiness, his own future. He'd walked out on Sylvie when she'd needed him most.

The professor had lost his daughter at Kane's hands. Was it possible Kane had pushed him over the edge? Was it possible Bertram was so desperate, so thirsty for revenge that he'd resolved to take from Kane what Kane had stolen from him? Was it possible he'd decided to kill Kane's daughters?

Bryce jumped out of the car. Leaving the engine running, he dashed for the police line. He had to find Nikki and Perreth. He had to tell them about Bertram. He had to find Sylvie before it was too late.

And he wasn't going to let the young cop stop him this time.

SYLVIE'S HEAD THROBBED. Her mouth felt dry and gritty as sand. She lay on her back in some sort of bed. A musty pillow supported her head, but she couldn't move her hands and feet, as if she was tied to the bed by wrists and ankles.

Through her lashes she could see outlines of windows where feeble light leeched around room-darkening shades. She willed her eyes to open, to adjust to the lack of light. But in the end of the room where she was tied, blackness still surrounded her, smothered her, beat her down.

"Sylvie? Are you awake?"

The voice was weak, but familiar. A voice she had dreamed of hearing. A voice she was searching for. "Diana?"

"Sylvie. Over here."

Slowly she turned her aching head in the direction of Diana's voice. She couldn't see her sister's face. But the white glow of her wedding gown filtered through the dark.

"Diana. Thank God."

"Oh, Syl. I'm so sorry he got you, too. I'm so sorry."

The man in the ski mask. The man with the broad shoulders and voice she'd heard over the phone. "Who, Diana? Who is *he?*"

"Vincent Bertram."

"The professor?" She tried to shake her head, pain erupting behind her eyes and shooting down the back of her neck. It couldn't be Bertram. That didn't make sense. "Why? Why would he do this?"

"There's a lot I haven't told you, Syl. So much you don't know."

"I saw Dryden Kane today."

"Then you *do* know."

Diana's voice trembled. With shame. With regret. Emotions Sylvie knew all too well. Emotions that clung to her skin, flowed through her blood and burrowed into the marrow of her bones. "Why didn't you tell me?"

A muffled sob rose in the darkness. The rustle of satin. "I didn't know what you'd do."

"What do you mean?"

"You were always so guarded. So aloof. Like you didn't trust me. I thought if I told you before we got to know each other, before we really felt like sisters, you wouldn't want anything to do with me. I was afraid I'd never hear from you again."

Sylvie's heart shifted in her chest. She wanted to

tell Diana she was wrong. She wanted to believe her longing for a family was strong enough that she never would have shied away from her sister no matter how ugly reality was. But the truth was, she didn't know how she would have reacted if Diana had told her the truth when they'd first met. Maybe she would have refused to believe she was the daughter of a serial killer. Maybe she would have run away to protect her heart. Maybe she would have denied Diana was her twin, even though all the evidence she needed was in her sister's face. And in her own heart.

She took in a deep breath of musty-smelling air. She couldn't say how she would have felt six months ago, but she knew how she felt now. Now that she'd risked her life to find her sister. Now that she'd risked her heart by opening it to Bryce. She'd already ventured to the edge of the cliff and jumped. There was no going back. She might have had questions at one time, but she had none now. "He's my father, too, Diana. And as much as I want to run from that fact, I'd never run from you."

"I'm so sorry, Syl."

"It's okay."

"No, it's not. I've always relied on other people to protect me. To keep me safe. And now look where I am. The same spot I've been trying to escape my whole life. And because of me, you're here, too."

Sylvie focused on the glow of her sister's gown, the gleam of her blond hair. Diana was the strong one as a child, the healthy one. She'd been the one adopted. Raised by a wealthy family. Engaged to marry a man who loved her. Yet things weren't always as they seemed. If Sylvie had learned anything in the last few days, that was it. "We aren't going to be victims, Diana. We'll find a way out."

"Professor Bertram has lost his mind. I've tried everything I can think of to—"

A metallic rattle cut the darkness. A door creaked open. A shadow loomed against the twilight sky, broad shoulders filling the doorway.

Chapter Eighteen

You have no idea of the horror I've been through. Weeks of not knowing. Months of asking why. Years of grief. My life is over. Ruined. And he will never pay. Not enough. But you will pay for him.

Sitting at the desk in Sylvie's hotel room, Bryce slid the letter back into its envelope. How could he have been so stupid as to assume the letter was written by Kane? Had he been that obsessed with the serial killer? Had he been that blind?

It seemed so obvious now.

He set the letter on the desk and started paging through the photocopied articles in Diana Gale's folder, frustration pounding in his ears. When he'd told Nikki and Perreth his reasons for believing Professor Bertram had kidnapped Sylvie and her sister, it hadn't occurred to him that he wouldn't be going with them, that he wouldn't be able to personally make sure Sylvie was safe. He knew that shouldn't matter, that he should be content that they'd listened to him, that they were checking Bertram's apartment right now along with his office, his wife's house and a vacation home along Lake Wisconsin. That they were using all the resources at law enforcement's fingertips to find Sylvie.

But contentment was an emotion far beyond his ability to master at this moment. And knowing that he could make little difference in the search even if he was with the cops didn't slow his heart or keep his blood from hissing with each beat.

At least they'd allowed him to stay in Sylvie's hotel room. At least here he could fool himself into thinking he was doing something to help. That in case they failed to find Sylvie at any of the professor's properties, Bryce could come up with an answer. A place to look that no one had thought of.

He skimmed article after article. Kane had killed so many women. The blond coeds he'd practiced on before working up his courage to kill his wife. The brunette he'd killed to send a message to Professor Risa Madsen and his failed attempt on Risa herself. Three different locations. All remote. All wooded.

The professor's cabin was the best bet. He'd probably take them there. But if he hadn't…

He paged backward, to the deaths of the coeds, to Bertram's daughter. A picture of Dawn Bertram smiled up at him, her face in negative, an effect of the microfilm machine.

Tearing his gaze from the girl's face, he focused on the article. Dawn's body had been discovered in a gravel quarry west of Madison. The police reported that she hadn't been killed there, that she had been moved.

He paged on. Through the story of one girl after another. Each story made him think of the family members left looking for answers. Family members like him. Family members like Bertram.

He turned the page. A headline about Kane's capture screamed across the page. He'd been caught just after the murder of his wife. Sylvie's mother.

An empty ache hollowed out under his rib cage. Kane's depravities had been like a stone thrown into a still pond, the ever-widening ripple caused by each murder ruining so many lives. Those who suffered the death of a daughter, a brother and sister. And those who weren't old enough to understand all they'd lost.

Kane might be Sylvie's father, but she was one of his victims all the same. Just like Bryce. And he could only hope that she wouldn't have to pay further for her father's sins. He could only pray she wouldn't have to pay with her life.

He focused on the grainy photo of Trent Burnell, the FBI profiler whose work had led to Kane's capture. He stood near a cabin. A cabin rimmed with tall pine trees. A cabin that might be still there.

Adrenaline spiked Bryce's blood. He skimmed the article, landing on the cabin's location. It was barely dusk now. It would be night when he reached Kane's old hunting grounds. He had no time to lose. Especially since he had a stop to make on the way. A visit with an old client he'd once defended—a gun dealer with a penchant for ignoring the required two-day waiting period.

SYLVIE BLINKED as bright light flooded the cabin from the naked bulb overhead. Professor Bertram was back.

He'd been in and out of the cabin over the last few hours. Checking to see if she was awake. Testing the ropes that bound them. Cleaning and loading a rifle. This time he was dressed in a black turtleneck and black jeans. He entered the room holding a pair of strange-looking goggles. A sheathed knife hung at his belt.

He'd refused to answer her questions in his prior visits. But that didn't mean she was going to quit asking. "What are you going to do?"

He turned to her, surprised, as if he'd forgotten she was there. Or maybe he'd just forgotten she and Diana were human. "It's time for the hunt."

"The hunt?"

Bertram nodded. He turned to look at her with sunken eyes. He obviously hadn't shaved since she'd first seen him, his chin covered in silver bristle that sparkled in the naked light. "He hunted my daughter. My Dawn. He tied her in a cabin. Tortured her. Humiliated her. Then hunted her like an animal."

Sylvie couldn't believe what she was hearing. "You're going to hunt *us?*"

He pulled a knife out of its sheath and held it in shaking hands. The light caught the edge of the blade, making it glint with cold precision. "It's what he did. And now he has to pay."

A feeling colder than the uninsulated cabin sank into Sylvie's gut. Diana was right. Somewhere between grief and bitterness and obsession, Bertram had lost it.

He circled to Diana's bed. Lowering the knife to her chest, he slipped the blade between Diana's collarbone and the lace of her dress and pulled it upward, slitting the lace bodice.

Sylvie fought to control her panic. She couldn't let him take Diana first. She'd been tied in the cabin for three days with little food or water. She was too weak to run, too weak to escape. At times when they'd been talking, she'd seemed confused, disoriented. She'd be no match for Bertram. If he took her out of this cabin, Sylvie would never see her again. "Take me first."

Diana thrashed her head back and forth. "Don't listen to her. I started this. Sylvie didn't even know Dryden Kane was our father. I was the one who tracked him down. She's only here because of me."

"No, Diana." Sylvie injected as much urgency into her voice as she could. Diana thought she was helping, but she was signing her own death warrant. "I just saw Kane today."

"I'm the one he knows best."

"Damn it, Diana. Don't do this."

"It's only right."

Bertram ignored them both, having already made up his mind. He sliced through the rest of Diana's dress and undergarments. He spread open the fabric, unveiling bare skin to the harsh overhead glare.

His throat worked as if he was trying to swallow but couldn't. Sweat beaded on his forehead and trickled down one gray temple. He averted his eyes, as if he couldn't stand to acknowledge what he was about to do.

Sylvie watched him, recognizing the battle going on in his mind. The man wasn't a murderer. The guilt stemming from what he was about to do seemed to be wearing him down. And if that was the case, maybe Sylvie and Diana could appeal to him yet. Maybe they could both walk away. "You don't have to do this. There has to be another way."

He cocked his head to one side, as if really listening for the first time since he'd walked through the door. "Another way?"

"Yes." She scrambled for something to say, an idea he'd buy into. "You can talk to Kane. Make him see what he's done."

"Don't you think I've tried that? I've tried for twenty years. But except for that first time he wouldn't face me."

"What if I asked him to see you? Diana and I can both ask."

"He'll listen," Diana added. "I know he will."

He paused, then he shook his head. "It's no use."

"Why give up before we even try?"

"I know Kane. If he realized you were asking on my behalf, he'd only figure out a way to string me out, give me hope so he could dash it. He'd just want to see me suffer more."

Sylvie chewed the inside of her lip. He was probably right, but she couldn't admit it. That would be giving up, consigning both herself and Diana to death.

She focused on the professor. All he could think about was himself. All he could feel was his own pain. On some level, he'd become everything he hated. And if he murdered Diana and her in cold blood, he'd cross the line for good. He'd become Dryden Kane.

"I feel for you, Professor. I really do. But you

can't do this. You're not like Kane. You're not a murderer."

"But I am."

His confession hit her between the eyes. "The officer in the parking garage?"

Bertram shook his head. "He's not dead. I heard a report on the radio on the drive up."

Thank God. "Bryce's brother? Did you kill Ty Walker?"

He looked at her as if he thought the suggestion preposterous. "Of course not."

"Then who?"

He looked down at the floor. "You should know. You found his body."

Sylvie didn't have to try very hard to remember the smell of death, the sight of blood. "Sami."

Diana gasped. "You killed Sami Yamal?"

"He was going to the police. I couldn't let him do that." He touched his fingers to his forehead as if trying to quell a headache.

"So he didn't commit suicide."

"I needed to buy some time."

Time so he could kidnap her. Time so he could kill her and Diana.

"I didn't want to do it. I didn't want to do any of this." A dry sob broke from his lips. He slid his hand over his mouth.

Sylvie was getting close. All she needed to do was

to keep talking. "See? You're not a murderer. Sami's death is eating you up."

"Dryden Kane stole my Dawn. My brilliant little girl. He doesn't deserve daughters. Not when he took mine."

It all went back to Dryden Kane. To events they had nothing to do with. A man they had no control over. "I don't even know my father. Neither does Diana. We were three years old when we were taken away. We don't even remember him."

"If I could make him pay without hurting you, I would. If I could make him sorry for what he did. But he's not sorry. He's never going to be sorry."

Sylvie couldn't argue with that, either. She had no doubt that he was right about Kane's lack of remorse. Her father might not even be capable of remorse.

But Bertram was.

"I know you have your reasons. But by killing us, you prove that you're just as bad as Dryden Kane. You're just as evil. How are you planning to live with yourself?"

He stared at her with dead eyes. "I'm not."

Setting his lips in a determined line, he slit the ropes tying Diana's arms and legs to the bedframe. Pulling off the sliced dress, he secured her wrists and pulled her up out of the bed.

Chapter Nineteen

Dizziness swept over Sylvie. She gripped the mattress with tied hands, trying to hold on, trying to steady herself, to keep herself from falling into panic. But holding on couldn't steady her. Nothing could steady her. Not with Diana out there in the night. Not with the professor hunting her.

She had to stop him. She had to get free. But how?

She looked around the cabin. The light Bertram had left on illuminated everything, relentless as a cloudless sky. Unfortunately, even with the light, she couldn't see anything that would help her. The cabin was pretty bare. Only the two beds, a table at the center of the room and a kitchen area with wood-burning stove in the far corner. And although there might be a knife or scissors in the kitchen or something sharp in the vicinity of the stove, she couldn't reach it, not tied as she was to the bed.

Raising her head from the pillow, she looked down at her hands. White cord of the type used for clotheslines wrapped her arms just above her wrists, tying each to the bed frame. She could hardly move her hands. There was no way she could work them free. She'd be willing to bet Diana had spent days trying.

Alarm blared in her ears and seized the back of her neck. Just the thought of Diana scrambling for her life, weak and naked in the darkness, made the dizziness start all over again. She had to find a way to break free. She had to help her sister.

She studied her hands again, straining her neck, her abdominal muscles shaking with the effort of raising her body from the pillow. She took note of the way the cord looped around her arms. When Bertram had tied her, he'd hadn't pulled the cord tight against her skin. Instead he'd tied it over the sleeves of her chunky knit sweater.

She let her head fall back to the pillow. If she could stretch the sweater and work a sleeve out from under the rope, she might have enough wiggle room to get free.

It was sure worth a try.

She turned her head to the side. Bending her neck, she grasped her sweater between her teeth and pulled.

The cotton stretched. Little by little, she could

feel it slip against her skin and out from under the tight cord.

She gathered more of the knitted cotton into her mouth. More slipped under the rope. She was almost there. Leaning her head back, she bit down and tugged as hard as she could. Her teeth ached. The skin on her arm burned. Finally, the sleeve pulled free.

She spit the dry cotton from her mouth. So far, so good. Gritting her teeth, she pulled her arm up, working the bit of slack over her wrist. Over her hand. Free.

Blood rushed through her hand. Shaking out the burn and tingle, she made short work of the rope securing the other hand. Then she turned to freeing her feet.

She climbed from the bed and moved to the kitchen area as fast as she could on tingling feet. She needed to find a knife, scissors, anything she could use as a weapon. She yanked open a drawer.

It was bare. She opened another and another until she'd checked every drawer and cabinet in the small area. Each one was empty. She would have to find something outside. She would have to improvise.

She raced out the door. The night was dark and her eyes struggled to adjust. Finally she got used to the darkness, the slight glow of the slivered moon through leafless branches. The hulking black pine and fir. Steam rose into the night with each breath.

She had to be careful. She'd be willing to bet the strange-looking goggles she had seen Bertram carry into the cabin were for night vision. He'd be able to see her long before she could spot him.

Leaves and twigs crackled under her feet. She flinched with each step, waiting for a hand to grab her, the crack of a gunshot, the sting of a knife between her shoulder blades. She had no idea how many acres of forest stretched around them. She wasn't even sure where they were. All she could see was forest. All she could smell were fallen leaves and evergreen. But it hadn't taken too long to untie herself. With any luck, Diana and Bertram would still be nearby.

She still needed a weapon.

Searching the forest floor, she picked up a heavy branch. It was no rifle, but it would have to do. She had no better choice.

She crept around a clump of bushes. Twigs scratched at her sweater and clawed through her hair. Even though it was nearing winter, the forest felt alive. Eyes were watching. Human or animal, she couldn't tell.

Beyond the brush, a clearing stretched black in the night. She moved deeper into the trees, deeper into cover. Her only hope was to stay in the forest, to mix with the trees. Out in the open, she would be an easy target. At least she could fight through the brush and thorns, at least she had shoes and jeans and a thick sweater. Diana wasn't so lucky. For Diana, the forest would be difficult going.

She edged around the clearing. If Diana was having trouble fighting the brush, she might be forced to stick near the clearing. And if that was the case, Sylvie had better find her first. Before Bertram did.

A scream shredded the air.

Too late.

Sylvie raced in the direction of the scream. She spotted them on the clearing's edge. Diana was on her knees, Bertram holding her by the hair. A knife blade gleamed in his hand.

She gripped the branch, her palms sweaty, and circled toward them through the edge of the woods. She moved as fast as she could, as fast as she dared. Creeping up behind him, she raised the branch to her shoulder. She swung it like a baseball bat, aiming at his head.

The branch connected. The blow shuddered up her arms.

Bertram released Diana. He spun to face Sylvie.

Sylvie swung again. "Diana, run!"

He grabbed the branch, twisted it from her grasp.

Diana stumbled to her feet. She ran, plunging into the forest.

Sylvie had to give her a chance to escape. A

chance to hide. She lashed out with a foot, kicking Bertram's thigh.

He grabbed her ankle and pulled.

She fell backward and hit the ground. Pain jutted up her spine and slammed her teeth together.

She gasped. She had to clear her head. She had to get to her feet. She had to run.

Pushing herself into a crouch, she looked up into the barrel of Bertram's rifle.

Chapter Twenty

Bryce swept his flashlight over footings that had once served as a cabin's foundation. Grass grew high around the lichen-covered concrete. A white wooden cross and a bouquet of battered fake flowers leaned against one of the footings, the faded shrine of long-ago murders.

He let out a heavy sigh. It was a good thing he hadn't called the police and led them on a wild-goose chase to Dryden Kane's cabin in northern Wisconsin—a cabin that was no more. He sure as hell didn't want to deplete the resources and manpower they needed to find Sylvie. Of course, they probably would have known better than to drive all the way up here. No doubt Reed had already checked out Kane's cabin as part of his copycat killer investigation. He'd probably known the structure was gone a long time ago.

Bryce turned and walked back to his car. Maybe

by the time he got back to Madison, Nikki would have found Sylvie. Maybe it would all be over.

He could only pray that she was safe.

He opened the car door. Taking one last look around the pine and hickory and glowing white skeletons of birch, he lowered himself into the car.

A scream ripped through the forest.

Sylvie. She was here.

Thrusting himself out of the car, he raced toward her. He pulled his new pistol from his coat pocket, holding it at the ready as he ran.

He moved quickly through the barren understory of pine and fir. But before long the landscape changed. More deciduous trees took over the forest. Their leafless branches stretched to the starry sky, affording more light. But brush began to crowd his path. Thorned branches of wild blackberry ripped at his jeans.

He was thoroughly out of breath by the time he spotted the cabin and the white van outside. He was right. Bertram had come here, to the forest where his daughter was murdered, to act out his revenge.

A light glowed bright around windowshades and through small chinks in the cabin's log wall. This wasn't the cabin owned by Bertram. He must have rented it. Or bought it with cash under an assumed name. He must have been planning this hunt for a long time. Maybe since the first time he'd met Diana.

Bryce's gut tightened. Red crowded the edges of his vision. He took a deep breath. He couldn't afford to let his anger blind him. He had to keep his mind sharp, his ears open. Sylvie needed him, and he wouldn't let her down this time.

He crept toward the cabin. Reaching the door, he leaned close to its rough surface. Nothing but silence reached him from inside. No voices. No movement. Gripping the pistol, he moved into position. Taking a deep breath, he twisted the rusty doorknob and shoved.

The door flew open. He lunged into the cabin, sweeping across the small space with his gun.

The place was vacant.

The scream he'd heard must have come from outside. The hunt had already begun.

He left the cabin, moving through the woods as quietly and quickly as possible. Sylvie had to be out here. She had to still be alive.

He wound through trees and brush. Stars and moon glowed in the sky. Shadow puddled under pine. Something caught his eye—a golden sparkle of hair. A white gleam of skin.

She huddled in a small copse of brush. White cord tied her hands in front of her. Makeup smudged her face and cupped beneath her eyes. She sensed him, turning hopeless eyes in his direction, as if resigned to death.

She looked so much like Sylvie, Bryce could feel it in his chest. "Diana?"

Her eyes widened, as if she just realized he wasn't Bertram. "Please. My sister's out there. He's after her."

His heart hammered, feeling as though it would burst from his chest. "Where?"

She pointed away from the cabin, through the thick of the trees.

Bryce pulled off his overcoat and wrapped it around her shivering body. He pulled the collar over her head to hide her blond hair. "Here. He won't be able to see you in this."

She held the coat tight at her throat and huddled at the base of the bushes, blending with the shadow.

"There are keys in the pocket that fit a blue BMW that's parked just to the west of here." He extended a finger, pointing out its location. "Drive to town. Get the sheriff."

He could see her nod, a slight shift under the cover of the overcoat.

"Sylvie?"

"Don't worry. I'll find Sylvie." And if Bertram had hurt her, he'd put a bullet through the bastard's head.

BERTRAM STEPPED TOWARD Sylvie, his rifle leveled at her chest. Eyes hidden by night-vision goggles and face twisted with anger, he looked inhuman. Insane. "Go ahead and scream. No one can hear you. Not this week. I've rented all the cabins around here. That's why he brought them here, you know. So he could enjoy their screams. Revel in their fear."

Nausea swirled in Sylvie's stomach. Revulsion. "You enjoy it, too, don't you? You really are like him."

Bertram flinched. "I don't want to do this. He has given me no choice."

Fear no longer rang in her ears, no longer pinched the back of her neck. She'd had it with Bertram. His self-pity. His excuses. She wanted to shove his words down his throat and make him choke on them. "It's time you stop blaming Kane for everything you do. It's time you stop letting him determine your life. It's time you stand on your own goddamn feet."

Reaching out, the professor clamped down on Sylvie's throat.

She gasped, struggling for air. He slung his rifle over his shoulder and reached to his belt for his knife.

So this was how it would end? Right here in the clearing? At the hands of this asshole?

Not a chance.

Summoning all her strength, Sylvie plowed her foot backward. She connected with his knee.

He grunted.

She kicked again.

He staggered back. He released her throat.

She twisted and ran, dashing across the opening. Racing for the cover of brush and trees. Zigzagging as much as she could to keep him from getting a clear shot.

Gunfire split the air.

She tensed her back, waiting for the bullet's sting. Waiting for the force of it to knock her to the ground. Waiting for all of it to be over.

But no pain came. Had he missed?

She didn't dare look over her shoulder, didn't dare slow down. She reached the edge of the forest, crashing through brush, jumping logs. She ducked behind a tall pine, hugging the trunk.

"Sylvie!" His voice was far away, still in the clearing, but she'd recognize it anywhere and from any distance.

Bryce.

She peered out from behind the tree. Starlight glowed in the clearing, turning the grass silvery through the leafless trees. A shadowy figure moved toward her. Too tall for Bertram. It could only be Bryce.

"Bryce, he has a rifle."

"He's dead, Sylvie. The professor is dead."

Dead? "Are you sure?"

"I shot him. I made sure."

She closed her eyes and clung to the rough bark, her whole body shaking. "Diana?"

"She's fine. She's hiding near the cabin or on her way to the sheriff. I gave her my coat."

She looked back toward the clearing, toward where she'd last seen her sister. It seemed so long since she knew Diana was okay. Moisture blurred her vision, turning the forest into a mosaic of light and dark. "Are you sure?"

"I'm sure. I promised her I'd find you."

And he had. She moved away from the tree, walking toward Bryce. She didn't know why he was here, why he'd come back. It was enough to know that he had.

Reaching her, he grasped her hands, enfolding them in his. "Before we go back, I have to talk to you. There's so much I need to say."

She held her breath and looked into his warm hazel eyes. She had no idea what he wanted to say, whether it was good or bad, loving or regretful. But whatever it was, it wouldn't change anything in her heart. She'd lived too long in her protective cocoon, afraid to risk, afraid to have her heart broken. And what had it gained her? A lonely life where she had acquaintances instead of friends. A sister who was afraid to tell her the truth. A secret of her own that had almost died with her.

She'd had it with safe. She'd had it with secrets. She'd had it with holding back. "I love you, Bryce."

He stared at her, as if her pronouncement had

shocked all thought from his mind. "I'm so sorry, Sylvie. I was shocked and angry and totally screwed up. There's no excuse for my leaving you at the jail. I'm so sorry I let Kane or anything else come between us, even for a moment."

"You came back. You're here now." Just when she'd needed him most. He hadn't let her down after all.

"And I'm never going to leave." He took her in his arms, wrapping her in warmth, holding her close. "I never stopped loving you, Sylvie. Not for a second. I want you to know that." His fingers trembled in her hair.

Or maybe it was the echo of her own pulse. "I know." And she did. She could feel the force of his love radiating through her whole body, singing in her heart, dancing in her soul.

He pulled back from her and looked into her eyes, a smile on his strong face that stole her breath. "I propose a new deal."

She shared a smile of her own. "Will I like the terms?"

"If you don't, you can change them at any time."

"Okay, what's your offer?"

"I propose we take our time, get to know one another, and then we talk about making things permanent."

"Like 'white dress and matching wedding bands' permanent?"

"The whole package. White dress, matching wedding bands and children of our own. A family."

Sylvie closed her eyes. Marriage. A family. The sheerest cliff there was. The most dangerous fall. The sharpest rocks waiting below.

Opening her eyes, she looked into the face of the man she loved, the man she'd never dared dream of finding. The risk might be daunting, but the payoff was extraordinary.

And she was up to the challenge.

Epilogue

Diana Gale clutched the loosely wrapped bouquet of spring daisies in her hands and took her measured walk down the garden path. The June sun warmed her back. The scent of iris and peony hung sweet in the air, their blooms framing simple rows of chairs filled with smiling people. A guitar's simple strum blended with snatches of birdsong.

Diana reached her spot next to the minister and gave Bryce a generous smile. Dashing yet relaxed in his gray stroller, he looked happy. There was no hint of his ongoing hunt for his brother's murderer, the man called the Copy Cat Killer. No sign of the stresses that had played out in that forest many months ago. His hazel eyes were so focused on his future with Sylvie, his handsome face so at ease and sparkling with hope, that it made Diana's chest ache.

Since the night Bryce, Sylvie and she had walked away from that cabin in the north woods, she had struggled to put her life back together. Never again would she let herself depend on others for safety and strength. Never again would she let herself be so weak, so vulnerable. She'd been a victim since she was a child, but now—no matter how difficult life became—it was time to stand on her own feet, make her own decisions.

Facing her own weakness and dependence had been hard. Facing Reed had been harder. He'd always been there for her. Protecting her. Taking care of her. And she'd always let him. He hadn't understood why she couldn't let him anymore.

She swallowed, causing her throat to ache. She couldn't think about Reed. She couldn't think about her own struggles. At least not today. Today she would push the worries aside, the thoughts of broken hearts, the shadow of Dryden Kane. She'd made it through the winter, and now it was time to enjoy the new life of spring.

And what better way to do that than by enjoying her sister's wedding?

Diana turned to look up the garden aisle.

Sylvie walked toward them. Her flowing white gown of silk chiffon wisped around her ankles. The sunlight played across the white lace bow in her hair. And on her lips danced the most glorious smile as she strode forward to claim her future.

**Hidden in the secrets of antiquity,
lies the unimagined truth...**

Introducing

a brand-new line filled with mystery
and suspense, action and adventure,
and a fascinating look into history.

And it all begins with DESTINY.

In a sealed crypt in
France, where the
terrifying legend of
the beast of Gevaudan
begins to unravel,
Annja Creed discovers
a stunning artifact
that will seal her destiny.

*Available every other
month starting
July 2006, wherever
you buy books.*

GRA1

HARLEQUIN®

Super Romance®

A GIFT OF GRACE

by Inglath Cooper

RITA® Award-winning author

In a moment of grief, Caleb Tucker made a
decision he now regrets. Three years later,
he gets a second chance. All because
Sophie Owens walks into his store with her
little girl—a little girl who looks a lot like his
late wife. But in order to get his second chance,
he'll have to ruin Sophie's world.

On sale June 2006!

*Available wherever books are sold, including most
bookstores, supermarkets, discount stores and drugstores.*

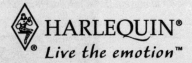

HARLEQUIN®
Live the emotion™

www.eHarlequin.com   HSRAGOG0606

If you enjoyed what you just read,
then we've got an offer you can't resist!

Take 2 bestselling love stories FREE!

Plus get a FREE surprise gift!

Clip this page and mail it to Harlequin Reader Service®

IN U.S.A.	IN CANADA
3010 Walden Ave.	P.O. Box 609
P.O. Box 1867	Fort Erie, Ontario
Buffalo, N.Y. 14240-1867	L2A 5X3

YES! Please send me 2 free Harlequin Intrigue® novels and my free surprise gift. After receiving them, if I don't wish to receive anymore, I can return the shipping statement marked cancel. If I don't cancel, I will receive 4 brand-new novels each month, before they're available in stores! In the U.S.A., bill me at the bargain price of $4.24 plus 25¢ shipping and handling per book and applicable sales tax, if any*. In Canada, bill me at the bargain price of $4.99 plus 25¢ shipping and handling per book and applicable taxes**. That's the complete price and a savings of at least 10% off the cover prices—what a great deal! I understand that accepting the 2 free books and gift places me under no obligation ever to buy any books. I can always return a shipment and cancel at any time. Even if I never buy another book from Harlequin, the 2 free books and gift are mine to keep forever.

181 HDN DZ7N
381 HDN DZ7P

Name	(PLEASE PRINT)	
Address	Apt.#	
City	State/Prov.	Zip/Postal Code

Not valid to current Harlequin Intrigue® subscribers.

Want to try two free books from another series?
Call 1-800-873-8635 or visit www.morefreebooks.com.

* Terms and prices subject to change without notice. Sales tax applicable in N.Y.
** Canadian residents will be charged applicable provincial taxes and GST.
 All orders subject to approval. Offer limited to one per household.
 ® are registered trademarks owned and used by the trademark owner or its licensee.

INT04R
©2004 Harlequin Enterprises Limited

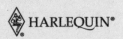

INTRIGUE

COMING NEXT MONTH

#927 COVERT MAKEOVER by Mallory Kane
Miami Confidential

Weddings Your Way consultant Sophie Brooks is good at her job. Love is another story. So when she crosses paths with Sean Majors while trailing a kidnapper, it's not just Sophie's life that's in grave danger. But her heart, too.

#928 RAPID FIRE by Jessica Andersen
Bear Claw Creek Crime Lab

Criminologist Thorne Coleridge suffers flashes that help him solve crimes. But are they enough to save his former protégée Maya Cooper from a roaming serial killer that may have connections to one of Colorado's finest?

#929 DUPLICATE DAUGHTER by Alice Sharpe
Dead Ringer

When Katie Fields travels to Alaska to connect with the mother she never knew, the woman is nowhere to be found. And the only man that can help isn't talking. If he had a choice, he'd be content just raising his daughter. Good thing for Katie, he doesn't.

#930 SECRETS OF HIS OWN by Amanda Stevens
Cape Diablo

Holed up in a Spanish villa nestled off the Gulf Coast, Nick Draco holds a secret that no one can ever know. But when a search for a dear friend leads Carrie Bishop to his doorstep, the truth will be revealed, and no one's life will ever be the same.

#931 EVIDENCE OF MARRIAGE by Ann Voss Peterson
Wedding Mission

After being kidnapped, Diana Gale realized she couldn't rely on anyone but herself for protection. Not her ex-fiancé, Reed McCaskey. And not her father, imprisoned murderer Dryden Kane. But with a copycat killer on the loose, it might be best for her to reconsider before it's too late.

#932 THE CRADLE FILES by Delores Fossen

Lexie Rayburn held a gun on Garrett O'Malley but didn't know why. Was he really the father of her baby girl? Could he help her find the people that took her baby? And did she really have amnesia?